BEST BOY

ALSO BY ELI GOTTLIEB

THE FACE THIEF

NOW YOU SEE HIM

THE BOY WHO WENT AWAY

BEST BOY

A Novel

Eli Gottlieb

Liveright Publishing Corporation

A Division of W. W. Norton & Company

New York   London

For information about permission to reproduce selections from this book, write to Permissions, Liveright Publishing Corporation, a division of W. W. Norton & Company, Inc., 500 Fifth Avenue, New York, NY 10110

For information about special discounts for bulk purchases, please contact W. W. Norton Special Sales at specialsales@wwnorton.com or 800-233-4830

Manufacturing by Quad Graphics, Fairfield
Book design by Brian Mulligan
Map by Mike Schley
Production manager: Anna Oler

Library of Congress Cataloging-in-Publication Data

Gottlieb, Eli, 1956-
Best boy : a novel / Eli Gottlieb. — First edition.
pages ; cm
ISBN 978-1-63149-047-7 (hardcover)
1. Autistic people—Fiction. 2. Congregate housing—Fiction. I. Title.
PS3557.O8313B47 2015
813'.54—dc23

2014048573

Liveright Publishing Corporation
500 Fifth Avenue, New York, N.Y. 10110
www.wwnorton.com

W. W. Norton & Company Ltd.
Castle House, 75/76 Wells Street, London W1T 3QT

1 2 3 4 5 6 7 8 9 0

For Joshua Gottlieb

PART
ONE

ONE

PAYTON LIVING CENTER WAS THE SIXTH PLACE IN a row Momma had taken me but neither of us knew it was the one where I'd stay forever and ever.

"My darling manzipan, I'm just so sure you're going to be happy here," she said that day with her red mouth that never stopped talking.

Then she started crying. It was raining. We were sitting in the parked car and I touched the glass of the window that was clear as air. Rain was exploding silently on the other side of it and this scared me.

"There's so many things I need to tell you and there's never enough time," she said and then wiped her eyes with her handkerchief.

"Momma," I said, "the rain."

"Please listen to me very carefully," she said. "Life has a song of happiness at the heart of it, but you can only hear that song if you work hard and are always a Best Boy and do exactly what you are told. You'll love it here, and Daddy and I will come on Visiting Day and call you on the weekends, and there's just tons and tons to do."

I said nothing.

"Do you hear me? Toddy?"

She was smiling with her teeth but the water was continuing to fall from her eyes and this confused me because the glass all around us was supposed to keep the water out. I made my upset face.

"Don't cry," she said, making a sound in her throat. "Please don't."

She shut her eyes and wiped them with the handkerchief again and said, "Remember this because it's very important. You are never alone in life. The happy song is always playing deep down if you listen hard enough. It's always playing *always*, dreamboat."

"I don't wanna go!" I yelled.

She put her hands on my shoulders and slowly stuck her tongue out and pushed her eyes wide open while moving her head around once, fast, in a big circle. I was thirteen years old and I laughed.

"Who knows best?" she said and winked.

"You do."

"And how do I know?"

"Because you're my Momma."

"And how long will I know?"

"Forever and ever."

"And how long is forever?"

"Just past eternity and turn left."

She smiled and hugged me with the warm front of her body and I relaxed like I sometimes did when she did that. But then there was a clicking on the glass by my head. A man in a white

smock holding an umbrella over his head was tapping his ring on the window. He showed his teeth and crooked his finger at me to get out of the car and instantly I felt the volts getting ready to burst and sizzle in my head and I began to scream.

The rain that fell that day is now forty-one years old but whenever it rains it's like part of that rain is still falling, it is. "The tears of God," Raykene sometimes calls the rain. Raykene is my favorite daystaff here at Payton. I have several daystaff but she is my Main which means she's the person I spend the most time with. Her skin is brown and her hair has a live-fibered feeling and she's very religious.

"You're doing the Lord's work," she always says, when she sees me doing my chores. Or, "It's the Lord's work," she says, when she reads something bad that happened to people in the paper. Sometimes she takes me to her megachurch where the Lord is so condensed that people faint and shout out loud at how much of the Lord there is. The preacher has a rich yelling voice and when the chorus sings it's like the bang of thunder that comes mixed with lightning.

Until recently, I was very happy at Payton, where I live with the other "villagers" in cottages with painted numbers on them arranged in a circle on a big plate of grass. Staff here called me the "old fox" and the "village elder." They clapped me approvingly on the shoulder and said, "Todd, you're the Rock of Ages." But then several things happened, and I stopped being happy. Then a few more weeks went by and I got even less happy. The unhappiness kept getting larger and larger till finally I was so unhappy that it was raining all the time in my head even in sunshine and wherever I looked all I saw were gray dots of water falling sideways across the view.

That was how I began to drown.

TWO

THE VILLAGERS HERE ARE DIVIDED INTO THE
Developmentals, like me, and the BI's, which stands for
brain-injured, like my new roommate Tommy Doon. There
used to be mostly only Developmentals here, but a man named
Damian Lands who is the president of Payton International
decided to increase the percentage of BI's. He said it would
make Payton "far more respectful" of "the range of human
diversity."

He didn't say that it would make his company eligible for a lot
more money from the government.

I know how to read, which not everybody knows because I
don't talk much. As for my new roommate Tommy Doon, he
arrived two weeks ago and I already dislike him lots. Also, I'm
afraid of him. Staff explained to him that if I get too upset I'll
suffer an attack of volts and he's been trying to make it happen ever since. He thinks it's funny. For example, earlier today
during Free Time I was sitting in my room listening to music

when I heard him calling my name. I got up and walked into the living room of our cottage.

This is what happened next.

"Todd Aaron," Tommy said loudly, not looking at me. Tommy hurt his brain in a car crash and is very fat. Also, he loves television and watches shows as much as possible.

I didn't answer, but converted walking into the living room into going to get my dinner. In the kitchen nook, the lighted box of the fridge is filled with sealed entrées the staff has bought. When I microwave them, the smell of heating plastic reminds me of the signs of the gas stations of my childhood: blue ovals, flying horses, yellow parallelograms.

"Todd Aaron leave the room now," Tommy said in his loud, dead voice.

"Please don't say that," I said politely. The entrées are labeled with Magic Marker according to the days of the week and I slid a Fried Chicken Friday into the microwave.

"Todd Aaron is *ordered* to leave the room now," Tommy Doon said, and turned up the volume and kept his hand on the channel-changing button of the remote control so that the frames of the television crashed into one another noisily. He looked over to see how close I was to getting volts.

"No," I said, in a slightly louder voice that was still kind of soft. I can't bear to push my mind back against anybody, at any time, ever.

"If Todd Aaron does not leave the room now," he said, "then Tommy Doon will scream in his ear as loud as he can."

To keep the volts in, I thought I might have to bite myself again. Biting my hand has always calmed me. The therapist here calls it "self-soothing." My palm has a big red saddle of scar tissue from biting, and my hand was suddenly trembling with wanting to be in my mouth. But before I could do anything else the microwave rang, and I opened the door of the little house of the oven and the light went on magically above my steaming food, and I relaxed.

"Okay," I said to Tommy Doon and walked slowly back to my bedroom carrying my food with me.

Dinner bubbled in a plastic boat. I ate it slowly at my desk, looking out the window where I could see other villagers walking by, returning from work. All of us villagers work at Payton. Work is "a holy thing," says Raykene. It's the "basis of our dignity in life," she says. My own jobs vary day-to-day and some of them I like and some I don't. My vocational manager whose name is Dave assigns me a job each morning. These are either on the Lawn Crew or Woodshopping or my favorite which is called Working the Line at a local high school cafeteria. The name of the high school is Demont Memorial. The noon school bell there has a noise like a heart attack. Then the dining room fills with students making a thunder-sound of excitement as trays slap on tables with booms and silverware chatters and laughs as it falls on plastic. All the sounds seem so much louder than they should be that it can make me afraid the volts will come, even if it's calming to "dish up" what the students ask me with a long-handled spoon or stab with a long fork at the hotdogs that float in hot water like doodies.

"Latest research," I heard Tommy Doon say loudly to me from the other room, "shows that you're a jerk."

I finished my dinner of fried chicken while continuing to look out the window. Then I scraped the hardened bits with a spoon, carried it back into the living room while doing "tunnel eyes" like I'd been taught as a way to ignore Tommy, and washed the dish out before throwing away the plastic container in the blue bin for recyclables. As I walked back to my room I didn't know that something even worse than Tommy was already heading towards me from the future. I knew only that I was feeling suddenly anxious and I wasn't sure why. I entered my room and did what I often do when I'm feeling anxious. I went over to my dresser and I reached forward to the individual framed photographs of my parents and I turned the photo of my father to the wall.

THREE

ALWAYS, HE WAS HITTING ME. HE DID THIS WITH his belt or the cold meat of his hand, sweeping it through the air while he made his frozen face of tiredness. Then it struck. You spilled your soup your milk your oatmeal your beans, he said. Don't talk stupid and You make me sick, he said. Stop making that face and You made your mother cry again you little shit and Put your tongue back in your mouth NOW, he said.

The hitting itself usually took place soon after he came home from work. Dinnertime and I heard the car cough in the drive-way. The slam of the front door went through the air. Then he was on the stairs, coming up. His feet stabbed the wood with bangs. He said something to Momma and went and sat in the lounge chair of his "study" that was filled with books and a smell of darkness. The drink was in a brown bottle by the side of the chair. The bottle rose in his hand. It attached itself to his mouth and his eyes shut while his throat made elevator movements. After he took the bottle away he blinked his eyes in surprise.

"What's up, Tex?" he said.

"Momma said it's time for dinner."

"Huh." The bottle rose again. He blinked his eyes again as he took it away.

"What did Andrew say today?"

Andrew was my counselor at the special needs daycamp. He'd recently told my parents that I was too "difficult" to attend summer camp any longer. I had gone to this camp every day for a week in the groaning yellow bus. The camp was held in a swim club where lawns with curling slides dropped you into a large pool of blue water filled with speeding bits of light. We sang songs together and played shuffleboard with long forks. We pasted sticks into walking shapes. Two days before, my parents and I had had a meeting with Andrew. They asked him to "reconsider his decision." They told him they would give me a "real talking-to" and that I would be a "solid little citizen from here on and listen to everything you say." Momma made sad noises in her throat between the words as she spoke them and she rocked a little bit while talking. Also she did White Fingers from holding her pocketbook so hard she pressed out the blood. I sat in a chair and watched my hands chasing each other while Andrew told them he wanted to talk to me about it just the two of us the next day.

"I'm asking you again," my father now said. "What did Andrew say?"

I rubbed my eyes. "He said he doesn't think so."

The sides of his mouth turned down and he made the noise in his chest like a dog.

At dinner afterwards it wasn't that I stuck out my chin in a way that made him angry or dropped my food or poked at Momma or kicked under the table. It was that I started crying and couldn't stop. The lightbulb made me do it. It was a white circle on the ceiling over us that made a buzzing insect sound which stung me in my nerves. Everything got worse when my brother Nate whispered the word "retard" at me across the table. This made me jerk my hand holding a dinner plate which flew for a second through the air and caused a loud, white starburst against the brick wall. Up jumped Daddy with a shout and dragged me upstairs to my bedroom by my collar. My body was still eating food in its mind even though my mouth was yelling things at him as he pulled my pants down and put me across his knee. I turned around yelling and looked at his face that was yanked towards its ears so that his yellow teeth were showing and his eyes were slits. It was his hating face. He made the dog sound in his chest. Then he started hitting.

But even when he wasn't hitting me with his hands he was hitting me with the way he looked or the words were leaving from his mouth that crossed the air and did the hitting for him. Every once in a while he would hit my brother Nate. Those were happy times. He would pull down Nate's pants the same way he did to me and then make wet smacking sounds against his bottom with the palm of his hand. Nate would cry while I put my hands between my knees and squeezed for joy. Then, as my father continued hitting, the warm feeling would begin in the pit of my stomach and rise slowly upwards from there.

FOUR

T**HE MORNING AFTER** T**OMMY** D**OON TRIED TO** give me volts I woke up and took my pills, like I always do. Every day I take Risperdal to make me calm, Lipitor to make me healthy, Paxil to make me happy, Lunesta at night to make me sleep, fish oil to soften my stool and a baby aspirin for my heart. They come in a bubble-packed roll, neatly arranged. The roll has the time and date marked on it in sections so I know just where to tear off the special piece containing all the meds for that part of the day.

The pills keep me always a little bit tired, but it's important that I take them because if not they might call a Dr. Strong. "Paging Dr. Strong," they say over the PA system, when a villager is about to throw a tantrum and needs to be restrained by staff. "Dr. Strong on the double," they say.

I filled a big glass with warm water and took the pills in a single swallow. Then because it was a Sunday morning and I had a period of extended Free Time ahead of me, I sat and did what I'd been doing for several days now. I thought about the stick.

Stock.

Stalk.

Stork.

The stick was a pointed stick that belonged to Mr. Deresiwicz, the custodian at Payton. He used it to spear through paper lying on the paths and grass. As I worked alongside him on Lawn Crew on certain afternoons, I was sure that if I had the stick, and didn't have to interrupt my walking to bend down but could simply whisk stuff off the ground and into a bag I had on my shoulder just like him, I'd be a person already on his way out of Payton and maybe one day live alone and even drive a car.

So I studied this stick, that was a pure pole with a point on it. Later the same afternoon, when Free Time was over and everyone was supposed to attend a talent show in the Main Hall, I walked across the empty campus to the woodworking workshop. There I found an old broomstick in a pile of wood. I used the special jigsaw with the skinny blade and the high humped back like a man praying and I cut the end off. Then I sawed the flat head of a nail off too, but quietly, and I gently hammered the nail into the stick and then filed the nail sharp again where it was flat from being hammered. This was a beautiful trash-spearing machine and I was happy at myself and I whistled as I cleaned up. When I was done I put the stick behind some bushes outside and went on to the talent show.

Except it turned out that it wasn't a talent show but a singalong. A singalong is held usually in the Main Hall whenever we want to greet new staff. The problem was that when I entered the Main Hall that evening and I saw who the new staff was, I immediately felt sick. He was seated at the center of a crowd of people in the Main Hall and they had just started the welcome song. It's done to the tune of "Twinkle, Twinkle, Little Star" and it goes like this:

Payton Living flies on high
Touch the earth and touch the sky
Walking tall and feeling joy
In the hearts of girls and boys
And today we welcome a new staff
Who will help us out to laugh

Then everyone applauds, cheering like it's the best, funniest thing they've ever heard. But usually during these songs I'm only mouthing the words because my mind is focused instead on the soda machine in the nearby alcove that is filled with clustering cool cans of Mountain Dew and Sprite and root beer. Sometimes, after events, Raykene will let me have one.

The new staff stood up. He had hair that was long in the back and short in the front. He had a moustache that drooped on either side like a picture of a Civil War general in a magazine. He waited until the singing was done and then he said, "Unh . . . this is the part where I talk a little, right? Okay, name's Mike Hinton and I'm from right down the road, in Gatesboro. The short version is high school and then what you call a non-starter phase at community college. Next up we got military service, which was two tours in Iraq, Twenty-first Cavalry, Second Battalion. Hardest thing I've ever done in this life and maybe the next one too and pulled a purple heart and a Bronze Star doing it. Anyway, after my service was over and I come back home thinking I'm done with *that*, I'm like, *Okay, Lord, where do I go from here?*"

People were nodding.

"So I began taking special ed classes," Mike said, "which

opened my eyes, yessir it did. But pretty soon I got to feeling like I wanted to actually be doing something in the world rather than reading about it in a book. Friends, I wanted to be getting my feet wet and my hands dirty."

He looked around and made a slow chewing motion like he was eating a piece of seriousness. "Bottom line," he said, "it's really important for me to be here in this community of beautiful people, making a difference. And thank you for your faith in hiring me." He smiled. "Ta-da! The end."

People applauded as Mike Hinton looked slowly around the room, trying to fork his eyes individually into the faces of people in the crowd. But when he got to me instantly the bad feeling deepened in my gut like on the roller coaster when it shoots upwards so fast it leaves your stomach still hanging at the bottom. Underneath his moustache he was wearing my father's same yellow teeth and eyes and I started whimpering, unable to stop the bad remembering.

My Dad was dead but he was back again as a speaking person looking out of someone else's face. My whimpering grew louder and soon became an uncontrollable bawling in my mouth. Several of the staff started moving towards me but the face of Mike Hinton was shining at me like from a circle of light in the middle of the room. He looked like he knew exactly what I was thinking and he was angry about it. He looked like I'd just kicked dirt onto the white cake of his life.

Raykene took me gently by the arm and out of the room and led me back to my cottage. "Todd, shush, now," she said. "You know how you get with new men staff, and how you were with Roy and Lebron. But you're gonna love Mike, honey, you really are. I've talked to him and our man is one of the good guys, like you."

She made me brush my teeth and wash my face while she stood in the door of the bathroom of my house, watching. Afterwards she came close and bent over me and the warmth of the air around her body went into me in a calming way as she hugged me good night. I got into bed and turned on the bedside radio. The stripe of numbers glowed. "Unchained Melody" by the Righteous Brothers was playing. I can remember every song I've ever heard. I can remember exactly where I was and what I was doing when I first heard it. Momma was a piano teacher and I'd spent a million hours sitting listening as she moved her hands over the keyboard and notes flew into the air and then gradually filled me up.

"Good night, sugar," Raykene said softly and shut the door. It was early to go to bed but staff made us do it if they thought we were getting nervous. Pre-sleep they called it. I did Pre-sleep while thinking that the way my parents died had nothing to do with how a switch on a wall threw light across a room but that it was still a kind of magic. It was a magic how they walked out of their clothes and bodies and simply disappeared. It was a magic how everything they owned suddenly lost its forward motion like a sailboat when the wind stops.

My Dad was gone. I'd seen the coffin. It was lowered on a kind of cloth band into the hole. Dirt fell with a rattle. "Unchained Melody" ended and "To Sir, with Love" began. Daddy wasn't coming back ever but I was nervous anyway. I knew that in one of the cottages nearby Mike was sitting wearing my father's expression on his face and making up something specially bad, just for me. I knew he was. I was sure of it. I started whimpering again, and stayed there lying in my bed until everyone had gone to sleep. Then I put my clothes back on and went outside. I walked across the dark campus till I found the stick again in the bushes and I held it in my hand. I couldn't bear to push my mind back against anyone, but this wasn't my mind. It was a sharp stick that could fly through the air.

I had heard where Mike lived and I carried the stick to the bushes right near his cottage. Then I stayed there for a while, bent low over it, rocking and making the dog noise in my chest like my Dad with my eyes shut.

FIVE

EVERYBODY THINKS THEY KNOW WHAT'S WRONG with me, but they don't. They think I'm autistic, but they don't exactly know what that means either. A doctor named Eugene Bleuler made up the word "autism" in 1911 though it didn't get used on anybody until a long time later. The last name of Bleuler sounds like it might belong to a fat man who's bursting out of his clothes with a pop. But actually he was a Swiss doctor with a moustache who was good with words because he also made up the one "schizophrenia." After Eugene Bleuler, no one thought about autism for a while because of being distracted by World Wars. But then starting in the 1940s, one person after another began explaining that they knew what autism was and you should let them tell you.

Not only do I sometimes read the paper, I also read the *Encyclopedia Britannica* too. No one knows that either, even though I have it under my bed. My Momma first brought me the Encyclopedia when I was twelve years old. I had just arrived at the

Clovis Center and she asked the director there to make a "special exception" and he said yes and so have all the other directors since. She used to bring me the *Britannica* yearbooks each year too until she died, Momma. Most people think the Encyclopedia is there to make me happy like a piece of blanket from childhood but I actually read it lots because the Encyclopedia has a voice that belongs to a man sitting in a room at a table who wants to calmly talk about every single thing in the world and it calms me to hear that. It calms me how he never gets angry or sick or makes the dog growl in his chest. It calms me that he only waits patiently for you to turn to the page so he can start talking again. I told Raykene about him and she laughed and said she was gonna call the *Britannica* Mr. B. Now whenever I ask her a question she doesn't know the answer to she says, "Whyn't you ask Mr. B?"

When I asked him, Mr. B said that the explaining about autism has gone on for a while and continued till today and still no one knows exactly what it is. He said this is true even though scientists are always having all sorts of what he calls *groundbreaking discoveries* about autism. He says they're doing a lot of tying of autism to things in the *environment*, when they're not doing groundbreaking. Meanwhile, there are the skulls. I like thinking about the skulls. They're kept in museums in places like Germany and France, and they're shiny because they've been painted with varnish by museum people to keep them from rotting in air which is called *oxidation*.

The skulls are from a period of long ago known as the *Neolithic*. Mr. B says that this was when groups of people first began having fun together, eight thousand years ago. He says they played string instruments, baked bread and kept pets. He says they did things with their hair to look good for each other.

The skulls have little holes cut in them. These holes are often square. Sometimes the cuts are perfect like the lines of a tic-tac-toe. They were probably made with a curved knife. Also the holes have *bone growth* around them which means the surgery was done on people who were still alive.

The question is, why? Why'd they do it? Who was the first person who said, "I know, I'll feel better when I cut a hole in my head"? No one knows the answer for sure, but Mr. B says that it's probably the first example ever in the whole world of someone being operated on by someone else to *let the crazy out*.

SIX

AFTER MEETING MIKE HINTON FOR THE FIRST time at the singalong I was nervous and I stayed that way. I carried it around with me like a fizzy drink I drank too much of fast, that was always about to make me burp. The pressure was inside me and pushing steady, even though I hoped it would go away. But it didn't go away, and then I met Mike again and it all got even worse.

"Hello, boys!" he yelled one morning, coming into the woodshop where we were making the famous wooden plates and bowls and salad tongs that people think of when they hear the words "Payton LivingCenter."

Mike stood underneath the wall clock, wearing a rubber apron and grinning. From that moment on I would always think of him as Mike the Apron.

"How we doing today?" he yelled.

No one said anything.

"Guys," a vocational staff named Joe said quietly, "some of

you here have already met Mike, who's the new broom here, and whose job is to sweep you malingerers into a crack crew." Joe winked at Mike and laughed. "Now, I want you to be very nice to him, and answer him when he speaks to you."

There was a silence.

"So how y'all doing today?" Mike said in a normal voice.

Larry, who was working alongside me, said, "Gool," which wasn't "good" but was close. Roy said, "You bet!" with a great sound of specialness, even though it was the only thing he ever said. Jimmy Nickle only looked at him, his mouth open with the surprised look on his face he carried around. I said, "Fine," but very softly.

"You dudes rock," Mike the Apron said. But though the words looked friendly in the air, they didn't sound friendly in my ear at all.

After lunch that day, I had an hour of Free Time and decided I would use it to take a long walk in the woods. "Todd," Raykene had once told me, "if you feel bad or think the volts are coming on, then you should just walk in the woods and scream and let it out."

Payton is surrounded by thick woods. I took the Pismire Trail. It went past trees and in the far distance I could see houses that had people in them though I'd been told to stay away. The trail around me was open and wide at the beginning and then it got more narrow and crowded with the branches of trees. The blue of the sky always seemed a deeper, richer color when you were inside the forest, looking up.

After walking for ten minutes I was in a place where no one could hear and there were no houses nearby. Here I could have my thought that Mike the Apron was going to be a bad man who was going to belong to the exact same category of badness as my father and that below his voice, no matter what he said or did, Mike the Apron was going to add more of this badness to my life every day.

I opened my mouth. Screams came out. These roughened my throat but I kept going. Stuff began pouring from my nose. My eyes were watering. The screams moved up into the air and mingled with air itself and were taken into the green dead rooms of the forest that went away from me at eye-level in every direction.

When I was done, I walked slowly back to Payton with a metal feeling in my lungs that made things quieter in my head. As I crossed the lawns I took a detour to the little white cottage of Mike the Apron. I stopped and parted the branches of the shrub to look at the stick again. As usual, I could feel my mind organize itself around the purpose of the stick. I could hear the whistling sound of it traveling through the air and then the hitting sound of it sticking into something.

I cut back across the lawn, opened the door of our cottage and marched through the living room where Tommy Doon was watching television. He began taking a long slow breath while getting ready to say something insulting but I ignored him and sat on the bed with my head filled with a funny new pressure. The pressure was because something had happened for the first time in many years and it made me confused and happy, it did. I'd just had an Idea.

PART
TWO

PART
TWO

SEVEN

MY PARENTS SEEMED TO LIVE FOREVER, BUT after they finally got very small and old and died, my younger brother Nate became my guardian. He lives with his wife and two sons in a house just up the street from the home we grew up in which is 744.7 miles east of Payton, beyond the mountains. I haven't been to the house but he's sent me pictures. It's a brick house with a big lawn. In one of the pictures, a dog is running in crazy circles on the grass. In another, a cat crouches, sneaking. If I look close, in the background I can see a sprinkler raising a claw of water. These photos are tacked over my bed.

But I've taken a pen and blacked out the faces of the animals. I can't explain why they frighten me so much but they do. Pets belong to the same category as typewriters that are filled with millipede arms which wave up and down to hit the paper and cash registers with drawers that open like laughing mouths with bills where their tongues should be and flashing numbers for eyes.

Nate comes and sees me when he can. He always says "see you very soon" but then a long time goes by and everyone forgets and it's six months later. Other villagers have family who live nearby and come almost every weekend. They have mothers and fathers who arrive in cars filled with the shattering glass sounds of children laughing and also sometimes picnic baskets and gifts. These families have outdoor meals in the rinks of shade beneath the trees on the Payton lawns. They go with their villagers to the Craswick Zoo where you can wear glasses and a mask and a llama will spit at you for money. They take them out for ice cream and visit the Londale Arboretum where the flower smells are so strong everything you eat afterwards tastes like an iris including steaks or french fries or even a chocolate malted.

When Nate comes we always go to the big chrome Pilgrim Diner which is near Payton and order the same thing. He asks me questions about myself and tries his best to be interested in everything I have to say. One of the things we also do is make sure never to talk about how much we hated each other when we were boys. We pretend just like Mom always said that "at bottom the Aaron guys always pulled together." Nate often has a drink like a gin and tonic in his hand as he says this and pushes the drink into the air at me in a kind of toast, even though I can't have alcohol because of my meds.

One of the specific things we don't talk about is April 13, 1968. That's the day I kicked Momma to the ground outside the ShopRite Supermarket in Taunton, New Jersey. I was eleven and attacking her from inside a case of terrible volts. The police came. People stood around with their mouths open in little scoops of darkness. Behind them big blue and red banners in the ShopRite windows announced a special on Starkist tuna at half price. Nate sat in the car watching, and I think maybe he was smiling.

We don't talk about the next day either, when the bruises on Momma's face from my shoes were hidden under powder, and she stood with my brother and me in the parking lot of a doctor's office, brushing my coat with her hands, holding me by the pointy twists of the shoulders and whispering that I should be a brave boy and a good soldier. "This is nothing," she said, pushing me forward with her hand in the middle of my back. "We'll be home in a jiffy, and then everything will be just like it was."

The doctor we were going to see was Dr. Smolan. Before him there had been Dr. Shtayn, Dr. Perkins, Dr. Farber and Dr. Mays, along with many others. Some of the doctors prescribed meds. Some prescribed foods. Some prescribed things like hanging upside down from a bar or lying in very cold water for an hour a day or eating pounds of vitamins that were stacked in little rows of brown bottles in our fridge. But Momma didn't seem to mind. There was always a new doctor with new ideas and for each of them she made faces in the mirror, painted herself and put on high heels and nice clothes. Afterwards she'd lean forward to fiddle with me while her fingers rearranged pieces of my hair.

But after the visit to Dr. Smolan, everything changed. She stayed in her bedroom for two days. When she came out her voice was higher, and she began running around the house a lot saying things on the phone and having friends over often for "conferences." In the afternoons sometimes she would take my face in her hands and look at me from up close while she covered me with her breath that smelled like bread. "You're my little piece of heaven, honeyfruit," she said. "And you'll always be till the end of time."

Everybody in the family seemed more nervous than usual, they yelled more at each other, and not long after I understood why. Because that morning Momma packed up my clothes and took me away from home to the very first of my many residential communities named the Astridge Foundation to "start your beautiful new life." Nate and my father said goodbye while looking away. Momma kept muttering to herself, "My nerves are bad." She drove there and almost had an accident on a curve, boom. But finally we were pulling up to a big pile of buildings in the distance with brick walls running around the edges that enclosed a park of grass and trees. Everywhere we looked people were standing wearing light-colored clothes with their bodies humped and bent and their faces squinting like they were staring into a bright light.

"We're here!" she said in a happy voice while she parked the car and got out.

I stayed inside. Through the windows I could see her making movements of her hands that I was supposed to come out. When I stepped finally from the car the grass and trees that were everywhere around me rose upwards in a single wave and I pressed myself onto my tiptoes to keep my head above the churning green water.

"Honey," Momma said and put her hands on my shoulders and pushed me gently back down to the ground, "not now."

Just then two young Down's girls walked by making noises and laughing. Momma began talking to me fast but I wasn't paying that much attention because I was watching the Down's girls instead. One was doing cartwheels in the grass and her skirt was falling over her and showing off her underpants which were very white in the sunlight.

I wanted to walk towards that whiteness and enter it like the ocean. It would be calm there. I would always have enough to eat there too and my favorite music would be playing with no one ever lifting the tone arm off the record.

But then Momma was hugging me hard and then harder with the tears falling all over her face which was upset like a baby's. Soon after that she was standing back up again and turning to the doctor who had arrived wearing a white coat and a big smile. Momma and he spoke for a while. Then he said, "Mrs. Aaron, I'm of the strong opinion that fast is better." Momma hugged me again making deep, thick sounds in her chest and got back into her car. It wasn't till she began to drive away that I realized something had just happened. The doctor no longer looked or sounded cheerful. He stared at me with a new expression on his face of a bored animal before turning and walking away. A staff named Tamara came up to me. She was very small and was wearing a T-shirt and white pants. She told me she was my personal counselor.

"I've seen a lot of them," she said, smiling, "and that was a beautiful transition, Todd. I know you're going to love it here. Can you follow me to your room, please?"

Something bad had just happened I now understood, but I wasn't certain what. I started crying anyway. But Tamara did nothing at all and only stood there waiting for me to stop. Finally, I did.

"There," she said. "See? That's not so bad, is it?

I didn't say anything.

"Come with me," she said, and she took me by the hand. The Down's girls were still tumbling on the lawn and I tried sending my mind at their underpants but it didn't work. The dust that had stood up behind my Momma's car was falling through the air and I wanted to touch the dust with my hands and then put those hands in my mouth. But Tamara was pulling me gently in a way that made me feel suddenly like I had to yawn and lie down, and because of that, I was able to forget about everything for one whole second, and in that second, it was clear I'd never go home again.

EIGHT

M Y NEW IDEA IS THAT I LEAVE, 'BYE. MY IDEA
is that I walk out of Payton and go home to live. I've
never thought this before. After I was sent away to the Astridge
Foundation, which was very bad and boring, there was Six
Winds and the Clovis Center and Persimmon Farms and Nos-
trand Bramble and then Payton LivingCenter, all in a space
of two years. Most of them were far away from towns and in
the countryside. You could just walk out anytime you wanted.
Every once in a while someone did. But not a Best Boy who was
always perfectly behaved and always tried hard to do the very
right thing.

My Idea is that I leave and go to visit my brother and maybe
live in his house or in a tent in the woods down the hill behind
the actual house where I was born. I could hitchhike or take a
train or plane there and do a job of some kind, becoming a "pro-
ductive citizen" which is what Raykene always calls me when
she sees me working hard. I could spend time just like I used to

as a boy, sitting in the cone of shade under the big tree in the backyard, flipping a grass blade with a hand and waiting for someone to call me in for dinner. In the process, I would stay as far away as possible from Mike the Apron.

Why did he frighten me so much? Everything frightens me but Mike frightened me extra-special because his teeth and sour eyes reminded me of my Dad like no one had since his death. He scared me so much that I quickly began noticing things about him. I noticed that he wore baseball hats turned backwards, had a white T-shirt with a leather vest over it and around his neck several necklaces with pieces of bone and metal on them that made a very soft tinkling when he moved, like coins in your pocket. On his feet were pointy cowboy boots. In his pocket, a folding knife, along with a wallet that was attached by a chain to his pants. Maybe he was chewing something all the time. Maybe it was tobacco.

People look like animals. A woman can seem like a cat walking on its hind legs and men in business suits can have fangs and the cold eyes of something that kills for a living. Human voices are also filled with the sounds of animals coming up into them from below. Mike was a coyote. He was hairy like a coyote and sneaky like a coyote. He made a call like a coyote that was lonesome and sad and left you thinking maybe he was a nice person alone in the woods and crying out for company. But like a coyote he actually hunted in packs and tore holes in the sides of his prey with his teeth and drank their blood like cherry cola.

Yesterday was the second time I was with him. We were taking a group trip to the Seabright Mall in the van. Normally a staff named Duane drives on this trip but I was already buckled into my seat when I saw Mike open the front door and get in.

"Everybody in a good mood?" he said as he started the van and the feeling of the motor came up through our legs.

No one said anything.

"No penalty for talking, folks," he said. "And air is free."

But still nobody said anything.

"Payton Living flies on high," he sang, "touch the earth and touch the sky."

Everyone stayed silent.

"Suit yourself," he said and then drove out of the driveway and up to a stop sign. He turned in his seat, looked directly at me and said very slowly and loudly, "Ba-doing!"

We drove to the mall through a flat going-pastness that was filled with the houses of the people who lived there set back from the road. Some of these houses had little farms alongside them with tractors crawling up and down neatly planted fields of corn and wheat. Geese flew overhead. Horses stood still in the sunshine. It was a picture on a wall that people lived inside of. A little while later Mike pulled the van off the main road into the parking lot of the mall and began backing it up into a space with a look on his face of indigestion.

"This goddamn thing has an ass like my first wife," he muttered under his breath. Then, when the van stopped moving, he said in a nice public voice:

"Okay, sports fans, file out nice and easy."

All of us walked in single file like we'd been taught through the main door into the Seabright Mall. The air-conditioning roared a moment and we were inside. The ceilings went up very high. The air smelled of sugar and salted plastic. Girls were everywhere. They popped their gum like pistol shots or talked into their phones and screamed with laughter. Babies yelled.

Microphoned voices spoke loudly from the ceiling. People looked at us.

People had always looked and in just the same way. But now there were almost a dozen of us together and so the looking was different. It went on longer and always finished with a shake of the head or a fake smile. I had on shorts, sneakers and a T-shirt that was pleasingly tight on my belly. Dr. Vauncy the dentist had recently fixed my chipped front teeth from when I bit a rock in a dish of lentils and now I had a "million-dollar smile." Next to me was Connie who I'd once touched the secret hair of in the dark. She was wearing sweatpants and her belly was bigger than mine.

Up and down all of us went until we had walked past almost every store in the mall. Sometimes Mike would let us stop to buy little things but I wasn't interested. For me it was enough to get off the Payton campus that I knew every brick of, every pebble and blade of grass, along with how it looked to see every-thing out of the corner of your eye or staring at it straight ahead.

It wasn't till I was sitting in the food court having an Orange Julius that I again remembered my Idea which I'd forgotten about for a whole hour. I smiled for so long I could feel the air-conditioning on my teeth.

Once the Orange Julius was finished, Mike led all of us to a nearby bookstore where he said he needed something and that we should all wait. I was a "champ" at waiting. When I waited, nothing had yet happened so everything could still be okay. Rocking helped. Rocking meant setting the waiting to a song in my head by moving forward and back on my feet and some-times actually singing something that was really little groaning sounds of breathing or I made my "wheee" sound if I was excited and rocked and smiled with my eyes shut. "Are you a horse?" a staff asked me once when he saw me doing this.

But back in the mall another thing happened that made me think my Idea was a good Idea.

When I opened my eyes from rocking, I saw a whole bookcase in front of me filled with maps.

That knew exactly the roads that led to every single place.

I stopped rocking suddenly and concentrated on one of the signs in front of me.

"State and Local Maps," it said. I pulled out several of these maps until I found the ones I wanted and then took them with me to find Mike who was looking at a big book with a naked woman on the cover that he shut with a crack as I came close.

"Painting," he said to the air over my head.

"Can I have these?" I held up the maps and the change purse that was heavy with coins from work mostly at the Demont Memorial High School cafeteria.

"Well, lookie here," said Mike. "He speaks without being asked a question. What's up?"

"Maps," I said and made my special smile that used as few muscles as possible.

"Oh yeah? Planning on getting your driver's license anytime soon?"

Mike looked around to see if there was anyone there he could get to laugh with him. But there was no one there.

"No," I said.

"Whatever, sure," he muttered, turning away.

All the drive home I kept looking at the maps. When I got to my room I piled them in a special place on the dresser where Raykene insisted I keep a Bible. The maps had crisp edges. When I opened them for the first time they sprayed fresh papery air into my face. My parents loved to plan routes on maps by taking a soft-headed felt pen and drawing lines along places they wanted to go. Momma packed sandwiches for those trips in wax paper that was the color of a brown cloud you could see pieces of food through. She wore shorts and a striped shirt. Daddy whistled happily. We were in the station wagon called an Olds 88 and driving down the highway to the Sandy Hook beach where the sun was a giant room you could sit in and watch the waves walking towards you and falling on their faces.

But that was a long time ago and now I was interested in another thing that maps could do which was much simpler: do what Daddy called, "Get the hell from Point A to Point B."

I found the map that had both the town where Payton was and the town where I was born years ago and I got a pencil and drew a 744-mile line between the two, again and again. I began doing the same thing every day when I got home from work and soon I created a river of lead so slippery that my hand would start at my Payton apartment and then automatically slide partway across the country and back home.

NINE

ONCE A WEEK WE HAVE A MEETING WITH OUR Main to talk about "issues." Raykene has been my Main for nearly six years, which is a record because Payton suffers from what one of Mr. B's yearbooks called *ruinously high turn-over* which he says is *typical of many state-funded institutions for the developmentally disabled.* But Raykene has stayed on even though many other people have come and gone. She carries a special book for the weekly meeting that she takes notes in. At the most recent meeting that was held in a room off the Main Hall, she was late and rushed in and said:

"Just never enough minutes in a day! So how we doin', Todd?"

"Fine, I think."

She sat down with a big loud sound of rustling and then she breathed for a few seconds, in and out.

"Whoo." She fanned herself with a hand. "Lemme catch my breath."

I looked out the window at where the world was, and, beyond

the mountains, the home where I had my very first memory of people leaning in over my crib and smiling in a way that showed their long, curving teeth and cold animal eyes.

"That's better," she said. "Now let's talk about things."

"Things," I said.

"From where I'm standing you seem a little bit worked up these days."

"I do?"

"Yes, and I got a good idea as to why that is. Do you?"

Before I could catch myself, I could feel parts of my face fall.

"Exactly," she said, looking at me. "You're an open book, Todd. From the moment you first saw this guy you were in fight-or-flight mode. I thought it was gonna blow over but that doesn't seem to be happening. Look, I'm not saying he's gonna be your best friend, but help me here, please. What is it about the man that makes you so nervous?"

"I don't know," I said. This wasn't exactly true.

"Well," she said, staring at me. "I'm thinking we better move on this."

"Okay," I said.

"Do you know what I'm thinking of?" she asked. I could feel the tiny heat of her eyes on my face.

"Annie Applin!" I said loudly.

She laughed a little bit, and said, "I'm-a call right now and set it up."

Annie Applin was the campus psychologist who always spoke in a low, calm voice that sounded like she'd made it fresh that morning, just for you. Mike the Apron and I met in her office the very next day. It was a quiet office. The way the sun leaned in from outer space to fall through the windows made it feel even quieter. The only sound was the noise of the ocean coming from a small radio on the floor.

"Good morning, guys," Annie said and smiled as she put down a Payton LivingCenter mug of coffee. Despite her calm voice she had a cap of fire-colored red hair on her head and smoldering red freckles on her face and even though I liked her she frightened me because I thought she could "go off" like a firecracker or volcano at any moment. "We're here, guys, to have a friendly chat and continue letting the two of you get acquainted," she said.

"Roger that," said Mike the Apron.

"Yes," I said and looked away from her dangerous hot freckles and stared at the floor. I wanted to talk as little as possible for the same reason I didn't want to talk too much to Raykene: because if I started talking I might by accident mention my Idea. And my Idea was becoming more important every day. As Annie began to ask me questions, I answered her by saying that everything was fine and I had no problems with anybody. When she asked what "fine" meant I said nothing. When she asked me who anybody was, I continued looking at the floor.

Then it was Mike the Apron's turn. I looked up in time to see his eyes bouncing back and forth very quickly between Annie and me over his big moustache. I don't like looking people in the eye because it feels like they're touching my nerves with their actual fingers so I lowered my glance.

"Todd's being polite but we know the truth," I heard him say. "I'm only here a couple-three weeks and I already got the man convinced I'm Saddam Hussein!"

Then he laughed his coyote laugh while strings of something whipped around inside his chest.

"Truth is," he said, after he stopped laughing, "my man is a straight shooter. That's the first thing. Also, he's got an actual brain on him and thinks for himself."

I looked up and saw him giving me a special dead smile in which he raised his upper lip while the rest of his face didn't move. "You think I didn't know?" he said.

Then he turned to Annie and said, "I knew. Todd's got a whole life going on hidden in his head. But do I freak him out? Yes, I do. That was kinda obvious from that first night. But he's gotta understand I ain't no Valda-mort. I'm thinking maybe we should try a little working together, do some vocational stuff and see if that builds some bridges." He paused. "You know?"

Annie was nodding.

"Building bridges," she said, "is always a net positive."

They continued talking but I had stopped listening. I was thinking of the films I'd seen of coyotes. I was thinking of how they walked kind of always like they were sneaking. They dropped their heads with their grinning mouths and they creeped forward. They were all always coming up behind something that wasn't expecting it and biting down hard.

I was surprised at a certain point to see Mike standing in front of me holding out his hand while in the background I heard Annie saying, "Affirmative behavioral support is the thing, Mike. We'll reconvene in two weeks."

"Fine," Mike said to her, and then he turned to me. "We agree on the plan to pull together?" he said. I held my own hand out in front of me, even though I had no idea what our plan was and I never liked shaking hands.

"Okay," I said, while I watched my hand go up and down like something caught in the belt of a machine.

"There, see?" said Annie Applin. She was smiling and reaching for her coffee mug as we left the room. "You guys are gonna have a blast, I just know it."

Two days later, when Mike the Apron showed up at our front door first thing in the morning, I found out what our plan was. It was that we work together experimentally on the Lawn Crew, and that we begin that day by clearing grass behind the septic tank. It was going to be a "bonding experience," he said, and some "quality time for us dudes." After he said these things while standing just inside my cottage he let his mouth fall open in a way that made me uncomfortable. I went to change my clothes.

Most people don't like working on the Lawn Crew and I don't either. You get hot and dirty and bits of grass enter itchingly all over your clothes and travel also up your nose and into your ears. Plus, using the tool called a "scythe" is dangerous. Many things scare me but scythes belong to a special category of scaring power. You hold the long curved blade by the two wooden handles and swing it back and forth intersectingly at the bottom of the grass as you cut it. You get a rhythm going and it can feel good in your arms but the blade is extra-sharp and is also very long. It's what the Grim Reaper carries, who brings Death. In the woodshop they no longer use power tools after Jimmy Hoffman cut two fingers off with a band saw and his parents sued. But they haven't figured out that the long, hooking blade of the scythe is just as happy to take away parts of you.

I followed Mike out the house and towards the long weeds behind the septic tank. Mike was very friendly at first as we started cutting. He called me his "little man," even though I'm taller than he is, and he told me that he knew some "bitching life lessons" he wanted to give me about "how the world works." Then his phone rang and he stopped talking and walked a little bit away and took the call.

I kept cutting while watching from behind the way his shoulders hunched up as he held the phone between his chin and his neck. I stared at his neck while feeling the big, swinging, easy power of the blade of the scythe in my hands. It sliced easily through the thick grass. It clipped the living green stalks and killed them. I began swinging harder, back and forth, enjoying the feeling.

"Little lamb," I thought I heard Mike say into the phone, "I like when you go baaa."

He turned back around towards me and gave me a wink as he slipped the phone into his pocket. He was smiling and shaking his head.

"Things just ain't always how they seem in life," Mike said.

"No?" I said, and lowered my eyes and kept the blade swinging.

"Take you," he said. "Now, I know you got some kind of allergy against me, like I'm born to be bad to you, but I ain't. Actually, guy, I'm looking out for you."

I looked up in time to see him showing the lifted-lip smile.

"Word," he said.

"What?"

"I've got a project that I need your help on."

"Really?"

"Hell yeah. That's what the call was all about."

Together we started cutting the grass again. The sounds of the two scythes at the same time are different than one. They make the noise of a large animal eating.

"What it is, I've gotta see someone right now in Peace Cottage named Greta," he said. "I'm helping her with her GED which you probably don't know what it is, but no worries. She's a little embarrassed about the, uh, tutoring so she doesn't want anyone to know. I can get behind that. What I was thinking was that you might just keep on working here for about forty-five minutes without me and then I'll be back."

"Back?" I said.

"Right where we started, which is clearing the grass. And by the way, you're doing a slam-bang job, my man, but while I'm gone you just switch to raking, okay? The other thing is to remember that what I'm doing is a secret." He stopped swinging his scythe and put his raised finger to his lips. "Poor girl would just be mortified if people knew."

"Why?" I said.

The finger went away from his mouth and the mouth frowned. "You see, that's what I'm talking about. You just mistrust everybody. What was it Annie was saying? Oh yeah, that you have to be less, uh, 'defended' I think it was. Well, here's your chance. You don't need to know why. I'm asking you to do me a solid for the sake of the community and one person in particular who needs a helping hand, and that's all you need to know. Stepping-stones, remember?"

"Stepping-stones" was something that people at Payton always talked about as part of the larger goal of "crossing the river of life without getting wet." Mike flicked his moustache with his fingers and made the smile.

"Okay," I said, lowering my eyes to look down at his boots that were covered with bits of grass.

"You just took a very positive step," he said, "and I'll be letting Annie know."

Mike stored his scythe behind a low stone wall and left for Peace Cottage walking fast. Peace Cottage had four girls in it who were the highest-functioning of all the houses at Payton. They worked in real jobs in the real world. They cooked at McDonald's, or did things under close supervision like restocking parts in a warehouse or they cleaned. A lot of them were cleaners. One of them might even have had a license to drive a car.

I raked the clippings into piles and as I did I thought of the girl at Peace Cottage named Greta. Her full name was Greta Deane and I liked her very much. She wore her hair at an angle across her head. She was tall and slender and she spoke in a funny way that made everything she said sound like a question because her voice went up at the end. The other girls in Peace Cottage didn't talk to me or even notice me but Greta Deane was very friendly and called me "Stretch" sometimes maybe because I'm tall. Also at assemblies she'd come right up to me and shake my hand like a man. Another thing was that she liked spending time with the animals in the fields which most other villagers did not. She especially liked cows. She once told me they were very sensitive like people and they spoke to her. What they mostly said, she told me, was, "We're here as meat."

I raked the lawn and thought of Mike's low voice moving around the apartment with the girls in it. I thought of his mouth slowly opening to show his wet yellow teeth. I hoped Greta Deane wasn't hearing him. I hoped she wasn't seeing his mouth. I hoped he wasn't making "baa" sounds at her.

A while went by though I'm not sure how long and then suddenly Mike appeared again. He smiled at me and he touched me on the shoulder and in a softer voice than usual he said I had "passed the test with flying colors" and that "a shitload of good stuff will happen" as a result.

I said nothing, and we continued clearing the grass until he told me we were done. When I got back to my cottage, staff had left a note saying that my brother would be coming to visit the next day and that I had the day off and should be ready. This gave me something else to think about other than Mike the Apron and I thought about being a little boy growing up with a brother until I went to sleep.

TEN

EVEN THOUGH HE DOESN'T COME VISIT ME THAT often and this sometimes makes me sad, my brother tries to call me on the phone almost every week. Often these calls are interrupted by his wife or his children or his work. Nate is an Environmental Accountant. I've heard him say many times to different people, "Environmental Accountants are in it for the green," and laugh. Nate taught me the word "eco." He has an eco-car and an eco-house. He goes on eco-vacations and he says the word "planetary" a lot. But Nate also told me that all he does all day is think about money for a living. Sometimes when he calls me I can hear a flat, hitting sound in his voice and then he usually apologizes and says that "work is choking me out." Whenever he says that I think what I'm hearing is the actual sound of money in a person's body, a stacked, walking machine of nickels and dimes called "my brother."

The next morning after getting the note I was sitting in my bedroom waiting when I looked out and saw a red rental car with Nate in it expanding in the window. The car crunched on the gravel and I got up and went outside to meet him.

"Tubes!" he cried, getting out and standing up, smiling. "Tubes" is my family nickname.

"Hi," I said.

"All hail the conquering Tubester!" he said and reached forward to hug me. I don't like when people touch my hair or clap me on the back but I like when they hug me. I like when they hug me really hard. I like when they crush me to their chest and build a wall around me that I can't escape.

"Can we go out to lunch at the Pilgrim Diner?" I asked as soon as he let me go.

He laughed and said, "Good old Tubes. Of course we can. But let me look at you first."

He held me by the elbows.

"Looking pretty sharp, you old jailbird," he said.

I was wearing brown pants and a white shirt that Raykene had recently bought me on a "shopping run."

"Thank you."

"And am I mistaken or have you dropped a pound or two?"

"I weigh two hundred twenty-one and a half pounds," I said.

"Sleek!" he said and let go of my elbows and looked around the front of the cottage where there was a little garden of flowers. "Everything's spic-and-span as usual. Your new roommate in?"

"No, he's out somewhere," I said.

"Just as well," he said. "Let's go inside for a sec, I have to take a leak."

My brother and I walked back into the cottage and he first came into my room like he always did. The room always looked exactly the same and he always said the same thing.

"There they are," he said, pointing to the photos of our parents on the wall. "And they would be so proud of you."

"Yes," I said.

"Okay," he said, "one sec."

He used the bathroom which made me happy that he was in my apartment doing that, and then he came out.

"Shall we dine?" he said.

"Okay!" I shouted.

From the very beginning I've always liked to eat more than almost anything else in life.

"Let's split," he said.

We got into his red car and soon we were bouncing over the gravel. Then we were entering the two-lane paved road at the end of Payton and as he accelerated onto the road I felt the small, even push back into my seat that always happened then, and I shut my eyes.

"So," he said, "how would you rate things just now?"

He always liked to play the rating game with me. Keeping my eyes shut, I said, "Eighty percent."

"Eighty percent is a solid B. We can live with a B. Hell, we like a B."

My eyes opened. We were moving at what seemed incredible speed.

"Talk to me, Todd," he said. "What's the latest with your people?"

"Um," I said, "they're all okay."

"Raykene?" he asked.

"Fine," I said.

"Raykene," he said, "is a peach in human form. We are very grateful to have Raykene."

I don't know why my brother said "we" so much.

"But there is somebody else," I said.

He was driving the car with little jerks of the steering wheel. "Who's that?" he said.

"A daystaff who is called Mike," I said.

There was a pause.

"And?" he said.

"He scares me."

My brother's head revolved all the way around so that he was looking at me, but only for a second.

"He scares you?"

"Yes."

"But why, Tubes?"

"Because I don't know."

"I don't like the sound of this."

We were silent for a moment and then we were pulling into the parking lot of the restaurant. We walked into the big chrome room filled with people who were sitting down before plates of food. I couldn't see anyone talking but there was a roar of conversation that seemed to hang in the air, apart from the people making it. My brother knew this noise frightened me and he shouted, "Steady on!" in my ear, and then he said something to the hostess who took us to a carpeted back room that was quieter.

As we were sitting down Nate said, "Don't get in between these country people and their food, eh?"

My brother once told me that he's very handsome. He said women look at him. The waitress came and gave us the menus and looked. I watched her looking.

"We'll have a bottle of fizzy water," Nate said to her, "and I'll have a Heineken. And . . ." He glanced at me with a question on his face.

"Yes please," I said.

"An O'Doul's," he added, "for my brother."

I can't drink because of the meds but I can order an O'Doul's non-alcoholic beer and pretend. Also, it has a tiny bit of alcohol in it that I can feel, which makes me happy.

"So you were saying," he said.

"What?"

"Napkin in lap," he said.

"What was I saying?"

"About Mike."

"Yes?"

"That he scares you?"

"He does."

"But why? Is it something he does or something he says, or both? You got me worried."

I wanted to tell him all about the bad thing that Mike the Apron was going to bring into my life and that I knew it, I just knew it. I wanted to tell him that his face gave off the same sour hot feeling as the face of our father and that he was a creeping coyote-person who was going to hurt the lamb of Greta Deane and sooner or later do something terrible to me, but I didn't know how to say that when I had no proof.

"I don't know," I said.

"Well try," he said.

I tried but nothing happened. "I don't know," I said again, but more softly.

"Hmmmm," Nate said, and then made his eyes small while he thought. "Say *something*," he said finally.

But I couldn't say anything at all. Nate waited with his eyes mostly shut and then they opened again and he smiled sadly and said, "I think I know what you're doing."

"What?" I said.

"No, I *do* know," he said.

"What?" I said again.

"You're trying to guilt me out, aren't you?"

"No," I said.

"Oh but you are, Toddie. And you're so good at it. But it's not gonna work. No, not this time. Not again."

I said nothing.

"Bro," he said in a soft voice while he leaned close to me, "do you think I don't know you wanna come home? Of course I know. How could I not? But like I've told you a thousand times before, we just can't do that, at least right now we can't. Now, if it was just me, then no problem, of course. The problem," he shrugged his shoulder. "Well you know the problem. It's Beth." Beth was his wife. "She took what happened to heart, and who can blame her—I mean as the mom, right? But I'm working on her, Tubes, swear to God I am. And she's softening."

"Stuffed shells," said the waitress, lowering the hot food that steamed to the table, "and a cheeseburger deluxe."

"Lunch," I said, mostly to myself. My brother was continuing to talk about how upset Beth was about "what happened" but I wasn't listening exactly. I had begun eating and was concentrating on my burger, which was very good. Also, what he was saying he'd said many times before. He'd said it almost every time he came to visit over the last few years. I always hoped he would finally say that I could come back for an extended visit but he never did. Instead he always said that Beth was the problem. Now that Mike the Apron was staff I wanted to go home more than ever and live in the woods behind where I was born or stay at Nate's house nearby for a long time. Normally I chatted a lot with my brother during lunch but knowing I couldn't do these things even now made me sad and I stopped talking.

"Look," Nate said after a while.

I continued not talking.

"Look," he said again, "Todd."

I kept eating silently.

"I get that you're upset."

I didn't say anything.

"But don't do this."

I continued saying nothing.

"Because pouting is only gonna boomerang back on you, promise."

I kept eating.

"And piss off the people who are trying to help you."

I stopped eating and looked at him.

"Like you?" I said.

He put down his fork and stared at me in surprise. "Whoa," he said. Then he shook his head.

"I'm thinking it may be time to give you another little rehearsal of the facts, my brother," he said. Then he made the same face he used to make when we were boys together in the backyard and he came with his friends John Latorta and Dave Mangell to torture me by pulling down my pants and pointing and laughing or spraying hair spray on my dingus to make it burn.

"What you need to be," he said, "is a little bit grateful."

I returned to eating.

"Grateful," he said, "that there's a person in the world devoted to your care who, by the way, doesn't have to be but is anyway."

I concentrated on my hamburger.

"Because this same person could easily, you know, leave you to the administrators and not check in at all, ever."

The hamburger was made of warm meat.

"And just pay the bills and ignore you, like most siblings of villagers."

It had little rippled pickles on it that I loved.

"Because that's what siblings do with villagers, mostly. They ignore them. But I can't do that with you. I wouldn't. You're my brother. End of discussion." There was a silence. "Understand?"

I was still silent and chewing my burger when he changed the tone of his voice and said, "Todd?"

"Yes?"

"It's your birthday next week, isn't it?"

"Yes it is." I said.

"Well I brought you a present,"

I love presents and immediately put my burger down and looked at him.

"Is it something to eat?" I asked.

He laughed and took a long drink of his beer. "As soon as you're done with lunch," he said, "I'll show you."

We finished eating while he talked lots and I didn't say much and then we got back into the car. He explained that the present was a glider ride and that we were going straight to the airport to do it. My autism comes with a special anxiety disorder that means I *react suboptimally to changes in the environment.* But the two times I've been on airplanes I've become extremely calm during flights and I like it. Nate knows I like it. He was excited as we arrived at the little airport and then got out of the rental car and stood a moment watching the big pencils of planes drawing lines in the air above the runways.

"We're gonna ride the wind like cowboys," he said, "and not burn even a single watt-hour doing it."

We went into the main building where we met Mel. Mel was

the pilot. He was old and very tall. He brought us out to the runway and all three of us went and sat in a kind of narrow canoe with wings. Another plane attached a rope to our plane and began pulling us forward. They rolled us bumping over the ground with little waves and wobbles and then we lifted off and were free. The plane tugging in front of us buzzed and the wind roared. Clouds that were moving high in the sky seemed to stoop down towards us as we rose.

"Is this cool," Nate shouted from behind me, "or what?"

Finally the tow plane disengaged and went away, trailing the steel cable behind it like a sperm. Instantly our plane eased up and began to float. It floated and floated silently in space, drifting. The pilot twisted the wings in such a way that it stood sideways up in the air and made my stomach lurch and my brother laugh. After an hour of drifting across the sky like a seed, the plane spiraled down and landed. It was funny to go from the drifting feeling of space to the loud specific fact of being on planet earth again.

Where I lived.

I got out of the plane and my brother and I stood there. He shook the hand of the pilot, who clapped him on the shoulder and said short, loud bursts of words to him that I didn't listen to. I didn't listen because I knew what was happening. They were having a man-conversation. Nate had these all the time. They often involved slaps on the back and lots of exploding laughing sounds. Sometimes there were winks. Instead of watching I looked all the way back inside myself to the little house where I was born and grew up. I did this often when I was around Nate. I did this because houses absorb people who stay in them by eating and swallowing them and part of me was still living there. The soft singing sound of Momma's voice was still moving around the rooms there. The soap smell of her arms was still hanging in the air.

Come here, house, I said in my mind and I watched the house walk towards me like a person.

By now Nate had finished talking to the pilot and was looking at me. He was silent for a few seconds. I could see his face falling while in the distance behind him a tiny plane jerked off the ground into the air and kept rising.

"You're doing it again," he said.

"What?" I said.

"I just took you on a glider ride for your birthday that was a hell of a lot of fun and costly too and you're doing it," he said. "Don't do it."

"Do what?"

He gave me a smile that made me stop remembering how much we used to hate each other as kids, and he said, "Doubting me. I can tell you are. Don't. You'll be coming home soon, Tuber. Just keep the faith." Then he took me by the shoulders and brought his face close enough to mine so that I could see the pink hoop of his mouth and his swimming-pool-colored eyes.

"Have I ever been anywhere but in your corner?" he asked.

ELEVEN

MIKE THE APRON BEGAN BRINGING "SPECIAL treats" by my house. He said it was part of our "new understanding," though I wasn't sure exactly which understanding he was talking about. The first time he brought by Good & Plenty's, which I like because they have a crackling candy varnish over a soft licorice center. The next time he brought over a large chocolate bar. Raykene is supposed to monitor my diet because I love to eat so much that I can get fat. My meds "stimulate" appetite. Also, I have high blood levels of triglycerides which is a "congenital" condition. But no one noticed that I was beginning to eat lots of sweets and I wasn't going to tell them either.

He brought over colorful patches you iron onto your jeans. He brought over a plastic flute and a spider of metal that walked when you wound the key on its side. Often when he brought these things Tommy Doon would glare at him from where he was sitting watching television and sometimes he would even stomp into his room and slam the door behind him.

One day he came by with a big cardboard box and said, "Okay, stud, something real special this afternoon."

It was Free Time and I'd been lying in my room listening to Neil Diamond on the oldies station. I love Neil Diamond even more than I love Neil Sedaka. When I saw Mike at the entrance to my room I felt something move in the back of my throat. I turned the volume down and looked at him. He said:

"See this box?"

"Yes," I said.

"Well, it's gonna change the equation."

I had no idea what he was talking about but since Mike was still pretending we were becoming really good, special friends I said the following:

"Okay."

"Yeah," said Mike, "you wanna c'mon outside for a little bit, I'll show you."

I didn't want to go, but I made myself get out of bed. Together we walked out the door past Tommy Doon who stared at us. I followed Mike to a field behind some buildings while he said quietly, "So, bro to bro, you did so good on Lawn Crew we're gonna do it again together soon."

"The Lawn Crew?" I asked.

"Just like last time," he said, and then he put the box down on the ground and out of it removed several pieces of plastic that he fitted together into something like a big flashlight with four propellers on its four corners. He put it on the ground and stood up.

"Ain't it amazing," he said, "what you can get online nowadays?"

"What is that?" I asked.

"Folks call it different things," he said, and from the same box he took something like a radio, with dials and sticks on it, and an antenna. He moved a stick and pressed a button.

"I call it the future," he said and winked as the little toy made a sneezing sound and the four propellers began to spin. This scared me and I jumped backwards which made Mike say, "Hold on, Sheriff!" Then as I stood there the propellers blurred and began whining and the plane shot straight up into the sky like something falling away in reverse, and vanished into the sun.

"What's really cool," said Mike the Apron, "is how the sucker has pinpoint control."

He fiddled with the sticks and the plane fell out of the sky, braked to a stop in the air right in front of us, and then shot away in a flat line towards the trees.

"Feeling *good!*" Mike the Apron shouted. "And get this."

Out of the box he pulled a little screen and angled it towards me. The screen showed two fingers on a pool table. The plane made another long curve through the sky and the two fingers suddenly became him and me standing on the wide, spreading green field, looking up with our mouths open.

"A camera?" I said.

"A for effort, bud." Mike winked, and then moved the sticks again as the plane flipped in the air and the screen abruptly filled with the blue of sky. "But not just any camera. This little thing is nearly a drone. I can do almost anything with it. I can hover. I can zoom, I can pan and wide-angle. We're talking military-grade toys for boys."

"Why," I said, "do you have this?"

"Because you can't ever know too much about the people you live with." He gave a laugh while the strings whipped around in his chest.

"You wanna try?" he asked.

"No," I said.

"Suit yourself."

He continued pushing the plane around the sky while I turned and walked away from Mike the Apron and went home. I wanted to sit in my room and listen to "Sweet Caroline" on my headphones and wait for the next thing to happen. I wanted to spend more time thinking about my Idea and how I could pull my home to me across hundreds of miles of space and wake up in my childhood bedroom again. I was almost back to my cottage when I heard a buzzing in the air by my head. I turned around to look and saw the Mike's toy plane sitting in the air right behind me with the metal eye of its tiny camera pointed at my face. A nerve of sight stretched all the way from that plane to the coyote-brain and yellow teeth of Mike the Apron and this thought made my stomach cold. But just then the plane kind of waggled its wings and shot away.

I went into the house feeling nervous and saw that Tommy Doon was inside my bedroom. When he heard me he backed out fast and gave a big shout like he was pretending to have hurt himself. But I understood what he'd been doing. He'd been snooping. He'd been looking for evidence in the case he'd been making against me from the moment we first met.

TWELVE

R AYKENE ALWAYS SAYS THAT HATING OTHER PEO-
ple is "deeply un-Christian" and that it's "never in your best
interest." Another staff named Chuck once said to me, "Hate
binds you more to the other person than anything else in life." I
was hoping not to have to complain about Tommy Doon to staff
because I never like complaining. But maybe it was time to talk
to someone about Tommy Doon because I was beginning to hate
him a little. I'd had many different roommates over the years but
Tommy Doon was different from the start.

He wasn't like Johnny Thewig who was very thin and nervous and hugged me hard each morning and cried, "You are
the one!" He wasn't like Brandon Aronowicz who smiled all
the time except when he began crying hard because he saw a
color he didn't like or a car with a human face on it, or Tom
Nassar who whispered to himself a lot and would only look at
you through a camera which he carried around with him, or
Steve Mothergill who always kept both of his hands in his hair

and would only take one out at meals to eat and then put it back again. Tommy Doon arrived in this cottage a few weeks ago and the main thing that was special about him was that from the moment he stepped through the front door he was sure I was trying to do as little as possible in life and would cheat whenever I could.

He was sure of this even though we have a chore sheet on the wall by the refrigerator in the cottage and a Magic Marker on a string and each day we check off things like cleaning the sink and emptying the trash and I do mine every day without complaining. But Tommy Doon who sits in his chair watching television as much as possible and flicking his eyes around the room nervously from his brain injury is convinced I spend too much time in my own room listening to the radio instead of salting Comet onto a sponge and scrubbing the sink which I don't like to do because it makes my lungs hurt from the bleach, or squirting Windex (lemon-scented) onto a rag and wiping the front windows of the house. All Tommy is supposed to do is mop the floors and broom the entryway. He's also supposed to beat the runner on the floor in the backyard once a week but he usually doesn't do any of it even though he checks the boxes on the sheet.

The main thing that Tommy does is watch me. He watches me very carefully. He watches to see when I'm feeling bad so that he can gloat and maybe make a lie up and tell on me. What he wants most of all is that I don't do well in life. I'm not exactly sure why this is. Tommy Doon is what Mr B calls *an implacable foe*.

Recently I was leaving the house and Tommy Doon tried yet again to give me volts. I was leaving to practice throwing the stick in the woods, where I had moved it from near Mike's cottage. As I crossed the living room past Tommy who was watching the nightly news on television he said something to me. I never watch television because it goes too fast and everyone on it seems to know each other already. But Tommy likes talking to me while continuing to stare at the screen with the volume up which makes him talk loudly.

"What?" I said.

"I said, where are you going?" he shouted.

"Out," I said.

"What are you going out to do?"

"Some stuff."

At this point Tommy Doon turned his head so that he was staring directly at me. His skull is shaved and he has small green eyes and thick lips. He raised these lips in the strained smile of someone struggling to push a difficult number two.

"So Todd Aaron has a girlfriend," he said and turned the volume down.

"No I don't."

His voice was deep with happiness.

"Oh yes you do," he said. "Why else would you be going out now? Todd has a girlfriend, Todd has a girlfriend, but what girl would be with you?"

"Goodbye," I said.

I walked out the door but I didn't slam it behind me. Instead I closed it quietly and then walked across the campus. I told myself I wasn't angry and I repeated it several times to be sure. It was just after dusk and I could see people in their cottages as I walked. The weak, moon-colored light of televisions glowed in living rooms. But often people in the houses weren't watching television. They were simply sitting in chairs with their TVs on while facing in other directions and staring at the walls. This was the drug Risperdal. Many of the villagers took it. I took it too.

It was the staring-into-space drug. It pushed a heavy downward hand through your head that made you so tired your mouth fell open and wouldn't shut.

I kept walking, headed to where I'd hidden the stick in the woods. Eventually I entered the forest and walked on a trail for a few minutes under the light of the stars. I got to where the spear was kept and I took it up and held it in my hand.

Around me were four trees that I had marked with little Post-its on which I'd written different names. The Post-its had blown away but I remembered that one tree was *Mike* and one was *Tommy Doon* and one was *Dad* and one was *Me*. Also I'd memorized where they were located so that even in the darkish light of the evening with just the planets glowing I still knew which tree I wanted. On this night the tree I wanted was Tommy Doon. The Tommy Doon who I could never bear to push my mind back against, ever. The Tommy Doon who had convinced his mother I was a bad person who "skirted his responsibilities" and never cleaned up, left a stink in the bathroom and had no friends. I pulled my arm back and using my body I sent the spear deep into the Tommy Doon tree. Then I pulled it out with both hands and I did it again. In the night, in the quiet of the woods, it made a satisfying deep sound like an axe hitting a log, thunk. I kept on aiming and throwing and then pulling out until I was sweating and breathing hard.

I returned through the starlit campus and opened the door to the cottage where I saw Tommy Doon watching a cowboy on television. The cowboy rode a horse that stood up on its hind legs and screamed. He looked at me and then said loudly to the television, "You do too have a girlfriend. You look sweaty like you just made sex with someone. Todd Aaron has a girlfriend and now I know he does and I'm going to tell on him!"

I went into my room feeling the nerve-strings yanking on the bones of my face and in my neck and shoulders and down my sides. I tried to remember what the staff named Chuck said about hating but it didn't help. Standing in the very center of my room I opened my mouth and gradually felt the electric pulling of my body come over me. My fists clenched and my face drew back until it was in the shape of a scream. My right arm rose without my control and my hand went into my mouth. My teeth bit down on the special spot that was rubbery from biting and tasted reassuringly like me. The volts were filling a room in my head. They were bulging against the windows of that room. I was biting down just a little bit less than breaking the skin. If I broke the skin and the volts came then I would see the white again and from the forgetting middle of that white I would kick at things until a Dr. Strong was called. But the windows held as the volts banged against them. For a long time I stood there with my hand in my mouth, rocking forward and back, biting the hatred in my body till it hurt, but not too much.

PART

THREE

THIRTEEN

S OMETIMES TO HELP IN MY CONVERSATIONS WITH
Mr B I do an Internet search. Most people don't know I
can do that either. But Raykene does. She says I can use it as
part of our "special understanding." She calls the computer Mr.
C. She says, "You asking Mr. B or Mr. C for that information?"
Then she laughs and shakes her head. Mr. C doesn't make me
calm like Mr. B does. Mr. C makes fizzing, electric noises from
the work of hauling information in from all around the world.
He says that no one knows when autism started but that people
were autistic long before the word was invented. Mr C has lists
of some of these people. He likes lists. He likes stacking information in piles. He says that maybe people *possessed by demons*
were autistic, along with the monks of the Middle Ages who
gave away everything, *spoke in strange tongues* and cried when
animals were hurt. He says that maybe the *Yurodivi* which is the
word for *Holy Fools* in Russia were autistic along with a woman
named Pelagija Serebrenikova who threw stones into a flooded

pit and pulled them out, one by one, and repeated the process until she grew weak, for years.

Then there was Wild Peter. *In 1723*, says Mr. C, *a naked boy was seen running along the edge of the Weser River in the town of Hamelin, Germany.* When the fishermen saw him through the trees they lowered their nets in astonishment and said German words to one another in their surprise that such a person could exist.

Soon the boy was captured sucking milk from a cow, and brought to a farmer's house. He was very small but he moved fast through the woods on his hands and knees. "Like the wind," local people said. "Like a squirrel," some said. "Like a goat," said others.

But he couldn't speak a word.

No one could understand how he'd lived through the cold German winters. The boy wouldn't talk and he ate only nuts, onions and potatoes. He had no name but people started call-ing him Wild Peter and he soon became a famous person in Germany. Then he was brought to London where the crowds gathering to see him were huge. One of the people who saw him there was a man named Jonathan Swift. But Peter wasn't inter-ested in what people thought, whether they were Jonathan Swift or King George. The king invited him to his home in London to meet his friends, but during dinner that night he got volts, tore off all his clothes, ate the food from other people's plates and then escaped out the window before being captured in a tree in the public gardens. After that, he was sent to live on a farm in the British countryside.

Wild Peter finally became one of the most famous people in all of Europe but he wasn't interested in that either. He loved music and humming and rocking in place. He loved standing outside in the farmyard with the sun on his skin or at night, watching the stars. He loved drinking gin. He never learned to speak more than a few words, but when an important judge came to see him when Peter was already an old man, he entertained the judge by slowly singing a song he'd memorized over the years. It went like this:

Of all the girls in our town,
The red, the black, the fair, the brown,
That dance and prance it up and down
There's none like Nancy Dawson
Then he died.

FOURTEEN

Payton has a list of "do's and don't's" for villagers called a Code of Intimate Conduct. It's written on a laminated card that is in a drawer of every dresser on campus. The card says, "Mutual sexual expression, which is private and between consenting adults, is a healthy and pleasurable demonstration of affection, intimacy and sexuality." Then it lists *The Ten Signs of Yes* and *The Ten Signs of No*.

Several villagers at Payton have girlfriends. Henry Mercer has a girlfriend even if she looks like a man. Ryan Hazonyx has a girlfriend with long blond hair which is always playing in the wind. David Pemberthy used to have Greta Deane as a girlfriend but then his parents took him away one weekend and he never came back. You can see boys walking around with their girlfriends holding hands. Or boys with boys or girls with girls. They gather sometimes in the bakery together and drink decaf and eat coffee crumble. They look at each other through the air and share their teeth in a smile.

The reason I got so angry when Tommy Doon made fun of me by saying I have a girlfriend is that I don't have a girlfriend but for a long time I wanted one, badly. I even made a bouquet of paper flowers many years ago in a craft class that I gave to a girl named Edith. Edith was fat and had dimples on her face and green eyes. "For you," I told her and looked away. When I looked back Edith was smiling at me in a way that made the slots come into her cheeks. She took the flowers and showed me the slots and said, "Thank you." But a day later I found the flowers dropped in the dirt near the recycling bins behind the main building.

I liked Edith. I wanted to talk to her and take her for a walk in the woods and to buy her a candy bar at the nearby convenience store. I knew we would never have a house together and a car to drive in and children to whom we would explain in soft, soothing voices that they were different from other boys and girls but still perfectly good people and maybe even manzipans. But I wanted to be with her anyway. And while I was being with her, I hoped she might help me do something about the wind in my pants. The wind had begun as a small breeze at age twelve a while after I'd left the Astridge Foundation and then increased steadily until it had begun to roar.

Momma knew all about the wind in my pants and used to help me with the wind by bringing magazines of naked women on her visits to me in various communities so that I could "work things out yourself." By this she meant masturbating, which is a bad word. We called it my "work" instead.

"How's work?" she'd ask. Momma at this time was a big hurrying woman with a pointy hairdo and heels on her feet but I knew that in her leather bag were pictures of ladies with their secret hair showing, waiting patiently to help me like nurses do sick people. For many years as soon as she arrived to visit Momma would take the magazines of ladies out of her bag and quick put them in the drawer of my dresser. Then she'd turn to me, smile and open her arms wide.

"My beautiful little man," she'd say and pull me towards her so that I'd feel the warm, living front of her body, "are we having a happy today? Can you smell a delicious hamburger and fries coming towards us from about twenty minutes away?" Then we'd laugh and go out to eat and I'd be in a good mood because I knew that after she left, a drawer of fresh naked girls would be waiting. These girls would always have the very same goal: to explain how nice it was to be photographed without any clothes on, just for me.

But after many years of blowing wind, the breeze in my pants had slowed and then mostly stopped. A staff explained to me that this was age, and meds. Mainly why I want a girlfriend now is to talk to her. I want to talk to her about how nothing ever stays the same no matter how hard you try. I want to talk to her about how when parents die they leave a hole through which you can feel the coldness of outer space. Girls are easier to talk to than boys. They let you hold their hands and they listen more carefully and they smell better and when you cry they wait longer before telling you to stop.

Connie is a Down's who sometimes lets me pat her bottom in the dark but I've mostly given up thinking about having a girlfriend. But then Raykene came up to me recently and said, "I got a favor to ask of you, Todd. There's this woman I want you to be an Ambassador for, okay? There's no girl Ambassadors available today and you're a natural greeter anyway. Can you take her around today and give her an orientation?"

"Sure," I said, and didn't think about it.

But later that same day I began thinking about it more. I'd just returned from the Demont school cafeteria when I saw Raykene walking across the lawn with a girl. I stopped what I was doing which was getting ready to heat up some lunch in the micro-wave and stood still as they came towards the house. Raykene knocked and stepped inside, sweating and fanning herself with a hand, and saying, "Too hot for words today!" Then she said, "Todd Aaron meet Martine Calhoun. Martine meet Todd."

"Hi," I said.

The girl had been looking down but now she raised her face for a moment to meet mine and I saw she had a patch over one eye. I'd never seen a girl with a patch over one eye.

"Hello," she said.

"Hi," I said again, and looked at her. Martine was very tall and very thin. She had long hair that was the brown color of horses. Also like horses this hair shone.

"Martine is the girl I'd like you to give a tour to today," Raykene said to me. Then she said to Martine, "Todd is one of our Ambassadors here, which is a special category of people who have been here a long time and are allowed to give tours. Normally boy Ambassadors give boys tours and girls do girls but we're a little short-staffed today and Todd is one of our most senior villagers and a total gentleman. Okay, Todd?"

"Yes."

"Martine?"

Martine said nothing and instead slowly raised an arm, swiveled her middle finger towards her mouth and then stuck it between her lips and began sucking on it.

"Show her the grounds," said Raykene to me, "the gardens, the Main Hall, the woodshop and some of the other places she might be working. Introduce her to people, okay?"

"Okay," I said.

"Great!" said Raykene. "I'll meet you both back here in exactly one hour. We good?" she asked Martine.

Martine said nothing but stared at the ground and swayed, while holding her finger in her mouth. Finally to no one in particular she said, "Ngggh!" softly. Raykene squinted at her for a second.

"I'm taking that as a yes," she said and shook her head a little bit. Then she left, fanning herself with a hand. The door shut behind her with a hiss. Tommy Doon had gone that morning on an overnight to his parents' so there was no one in the house. I stood for a while listening to the sounds of water gurgling in pipes. Something ticked inside the wall like a clock.

"Do you talk?" I asked.

Martine took her middle finger out of her mouth. Her face looked tired.

"Only if I want to," she said.

"Hello," I said.

"I shouldn't be here," she said.

"Payton is nice," I said.

She looked at me with the eye.

"No it's not," she said.

"Are there parts of the campus you want to see more than others?" I asked, because I remembered that this was what Ambassadors were supposed to say.

"I'm too high-functioning to be here, but my mother said I had to because I have intrac"—her mouth caught up on one side—"table problems. But she's wrong, as usual."

"We have bingo every Friday night in the Main Hall," I said.

"They're hateful."

"Who?"

"My parents."

"I wish my Momma was still alive," I said.

"You've gotta be kidding."

"I miss her."

She snorted and rolled the one eye. "What's your die?"

"My what?"

"Diagnosis."

"I have autism and anxiety disorder. Also I'm developmentally disabled," I said.

She shut her eye and in a fast, bored voice she said, "First they thought I was an Aspie, and then they thought I was an Addie. I had six different syndromes at the same time, plus being depressed. But it was all a lie anyway because they knew I had brain damage from being pushed out of a car when I was a girl."

Her eye opened. "You're kinda fat."

"What?"

"So are you taking me on a tour or not?"

I couldn't follow what she was saying and I felt my head lightly moving to and fro as I tried to look at the words going by quickly, zoom.

"Yes," I said finally, "a tour."

"Okay let's go."

We walked out the door and I began by slowly walking with her to the cottages. Each one had something special about it that you would only know if you'd been here a long time. She was staying in cottage number seven. It had a sewing machine in it. I told her that.

"I thought every cottage had a sewing machine," she said. "What does yours have that's special?"

"A back door," I said, "and a big TV."

We cut across the main lawn to the library. It was a little darkened building and I turned on the lights.

"Out the windows you can see Peace Cottage," I said, "where if you're high-functioning you stay and maybe even work at McDonald's."

She looked at me with her one gray eye.

"Do I seem disturbed to you?" she said.

"I don't know."

"My father thinks I'm making it up. Do you know how I convinced him I wasn't making it up?"

"No."

She tapped the patch over her eye. I thought it was soft but it was actually a hard shell because it made a hollow sound.

"That's how."

"Sometimes we also play Monopoly here on the weekends," I said and pointed to a wooden table.

"Actually I poked it out with a rock."

"You can take DVDs out on a two-day loan," I said. "And there's also a magazine rack."

"Don't you think that's a sad story?"

I felt my eyebrows pulling together.

"I guess."

"Or how about this one: I had a brother who died. I think maybe someone killed him. That's not true. My brain damage from falling out of a car? That's not true either. I jumped. Why do you wear your hair so long? You look old."

"Do you want to see the horses?" I said.

"You're funny," she said.

"There's one named Bob," I said.

"A horse named Bob? Yes I do."

As we walked across another lawn to the barn I realized I wasn't only nervous but I was also excited. She made me excited because she talked fast and I didn't know what she was going to say next. Also she was a tall person, almost as tall as me. Also she was a girl and even if the wind in my pants barely blew anymore, still I wanted a girlfriend. The excitement made me talk more than I had in a long time.

"This is Zoysia grass we're walking on," I said. "It comes from the Philippines."

She laughed and said, "Have you always been so tall?"

I said nothing.

"You know lots of junk," she added.

Then her face stopped what it was doing and yanked up on one side and her lips pushed forward and her tongue stuck all the way out of her mouth. She held one hand up in the air.

"Are you—" I started to say.

She shook her head like she couldn't speak. Her face began to get purple. But after a moment her face suddenly relaxed, her arm fell and she let out a breath.

"I can't *stand* those!" she said. "I get them at least once a day. It's from my crash."

"What?"

"Seizures," she said. "Sometimes you feel like you have to pee when you get them. Where's the nearest bathroom?"

I took her to a bathroom in a nearby building. She went in while I waited outside and then came out a minute later, smiling.

"Better," she said.

After I took her to meet Bob and the other horses I showed her the Main Hall where we had the singalongs. I showed her the painting studio and the bakery and the woodshop. I always introduced her to people inside the places by saying, "This is Martine and I'm her Ambassador. She's brand-new."

Sometimes she would shake people's hands, and sometimes she wouldn't. Sometimes she would act very scared and look at the ground and other times she would laugh loudly when the person I'd introduced her to said something like, "How are you?"

Finally we were done and I'd shown her everything I could think of. I was tired and happy. I said, "We're supposed to be back to meet Raykene at the cottage soon."

She looked at me with the eye.

"You really should cut your hair."

I reached up and touched it where it hung off my head.

"This?"

She looked up over my shoulder and made a confused face. "Do you know," she said, "there's been this kind of weird metal hummingbird thing in the air following us for the last few minutes?"

FIFTEEN

MIKE THE APRON CAME UP TO ME LATER THAT day, as I was walking across the lawn. I saw the mouth moving around below the striped coyote beard and moustache before I heard the words.

"Well, if it ain't Romeo," he said.

"Hello."

"You have fun?"

"When?"

"With the girl?"

"Which girl?"

"Don't play dumb," he said and frowned and forked his fingers and stabbed them towards his face. "With the eyepatch, guy."

"Martine."

"I know her name. Smart as a whip, according to her papers."

I shrugged my shoulders.

"A real talker too," he said. "Not that I heard all that much. But I could see that mouth moving from far off."

I thought of the stick in the woods, hidden in a fold of green earth. I thought of the way the scythe hissed and gobbled the grass when I swung it. I was trying not to be too frightened of Mike the Apron. But he was looking at me in a way that made me uncomfortable.

"You going to singalong tonight for the new staff?" he asked.

"I don't know," I said.

"You throwing a little shade at me maybe?"

"What?"

Mike looked around again to see if there was anybody nearby. He said, "I really like you, Todd, you know that, right?"

"I guess," I said.

"We're all family, here," he said and put his arm around me and drew me close enough so that I could smell the meat-cloud of his breath. "But I want you to remember that you and me, we have a special understanding. You do stuff for me and I do stuff for you, and it's a beautiful thing. That's what makes us," he said, pulling his lips back so that I saw his teeth covered with a kind of yellow rust, "brothers."

"Right," I said.

"Good man," he said, and then to my relief he turned to walk away and I could hear his laughing and snorting as it dwindled into the distance.

I went back to my house, ignored Tommy Doon who was getting ready to say something, took my meds and went to bed. The next morning I worked in the woodshop and during Free Time I walked in the woods. The trees with their long necks and big heads went sideways past my eyes like they always did but I didn't yell. I thought instead. What I thought was that something interesting was happening inside me, and that something was that I wanted to spend more time with Martine Calhoun. I was thinking that it was fun to be around someone who spoke to you out of the surprise places in conversation and had a girl-voice like a bunch of warm hands that pleasantly handled your insides. I couldn't remember having my insides handled like this by someone for a very long time.

Over the next few days, I began looking for Martine whenever I walked outside. I did this by constantly sending my glance out across the campus to see if there was a tall person walking. In woodshop, or from the van leaving for the Demont cafeteria, I hoped I'd see her. Even when I was alone and listening to music on my bed I'd find her stepping out of the voices of the Beach Boys or Herb Alpert and the Tijuana Brass or especially Neil Diamond and coming up to me and into my thoughts like a woman walking out of a lake.

Then one evening while I was crossing a lawn on the way to bingo, I saw her moving very slowly from far away. I immediately changed my direction to meet her. As I got closer I saw that her hair was funny. I realized that it had been cut. Actually it had been kind of chopped. Also her face seemed very tired and hung from her head in a way I thought I recognized. As I watched, I saw her mouth drop open. I recognized that too.

I went over to her.

"Hi," I said. She stopped walking and her one eye went slowly sideways and then met mine. It took a few seconds while her brain did the work of recognizing me. Then she blinked.

"Hello," she said softly.

"How are you, Martine?" I asked.

"Dead," she said.

There were other people walking by and I didn't want them to hear what we were saying. I leaned closer.

"What?" I said.

"I feel," she said very slowly, "like a parking lot."

"Risperdal," I said softly.

"I didn't know I could feel this way," she said.

"Risperdal," I said, louder.

"What?"

"The red one."

"Red what?"

"The pill."

"I'm taking all new meds."

"At the beginning," I said, "you're tired a lot."

"Does it get better?"

I put my hand out flat in the air and then waggled it like I'd seen people do to mean "so-so."

"Maybe a little," I said.

"Unh," she said. "I've been on lots of different stuff. But not like this."

"I know," I said.

"I've been in a lot of places too," she said.

"Me too."

"But not like this."

"I've been at Payton for more than forty years," I said.

"I mean people here are really sick."

"I'm the 'grand old man' of Payton."

The eye turned tiredly to me.

"You're old all right," she said.

"Are you going to bingo?"

"Only because they told me I have to."

"Do you want to sit next to me?"

"Maybe," she said. And then she added, "But I'm going to get off."

"What?"

"The Rasperdoll."

"What?" I said again slowly. We were still standing there.

"I'm gonna stop taking it."

I didn't know what she was saying exactly.

"Stop taking it?" I repeated.

"Now that I know what's making me feel so bad, yes I am."

"Um," I said, as we started walking again.

"Because if I take it anymore," she said, "I'll die. I'll just go away and I'll be dead."

"I don't want that," I said.

The eye fixed on me and squinted a little bit.

"Aw shucks," she said. We were getting close to the Main Hall and I could see people moving through the lighted windows, playing bingo.

"You wanna stop taking pills?" I repeated as we walked. The idea of doing this had never occurred to me. I was a Best Boy who did everything I was supposed to do down to the last detail and always had.

"Yes, I do," she said. "But I'm a newbie so they're watching me kinda closely."

"They sometimes watch me too," I said, because I remembered that every once in a while someone from staff came in to "monitor" me taking my meds. Plus, once a month we had our blood draws and they checked our meds that way also. But no one had to monitor me taking my pills every day. I did it just because it was the Law.

"Doesn't matter," she said. She looked at me and smiled mysteriously. "I got ways."

"Ways?"

She didn't say anything and we kept walking. A year or so ago I'd told my brother about Risperdal making me feel thick inside.

He'd phoned to Payton to have them change me to another drug that is called Abilify. But Abilify wasn't on the list, they told him, so it would cost him 450 extra dollars a month for them to give it to me. After this Nate told me that he would think about it but he didn't mention it again. Maybe this is because he's an accountant and thinks "about money for a living." I'd gotten used to the Risperdal but I didn't like it. But I couldn't imagine not taking it. I was supposed to take it. There wasn't anyone who didn't know I was supposed to take it. They all took it too.

"Ways?" I said again.

She didn't say anything but the eye caught mine and she smiled a little. We were walking up the concrete path to the front door of the Bingo Hall, moving slowly and steadily. I was watching our feet take steps together, attached at the end of very long legs. I was trying not to notice the hottish coldish feelings that were moving through me of wanting to be alone with Martine in a room. These feelings were especially strong in the back of my throat, which wanted to say words, and in my jaws that wanted to bite and chew. For the first time in years, there was a sudden gust of wind in my pants.

"I can teach you how to pretend," she said.

"Pretend what?"

She opened the door to the Main Hall where the bingo was happening and a waiting wave of sound fell over us.

"Pretend to take the pills," she said loudly.

"What?" I shouted, because I wasn't sure what I'd heard.

She winked and made round lips like someone blowing a smoke ring and gave a sound: "Whoooo!" But it was hard to hear because the room was deafening. People sat at long tables yelling and groaning. Some waved their arms, while the woman onstage cranked a wire basket that made a hammering of wooden balls against the metal parts and another woman announced numbers and letters in a huge, microphoned voice from the ceiling.

We sat down next to each other at a table and I said, "Unh," under my breath from the violence of the sounds in the air and the strange thing she had just told me about the pills and the feelings building in my throat and my pants. A staff gave us bingo cards and pencils. Bingo is easy. You just make an *x* in the box that they announce and if you get a row across the page they give you a prize of a small stuffed animal, a comb, a CD or a bar of soap.

As we began playing my eyes rested on Martine's face. It was from inside this face that she'd looked at me and also from where the words had come that moved my insides so pleasantly. A few minutes went by with me doing this while playing bingo. Then behind her face in the blur of the moving background I saw another face that I recognized. I tried keeping it in the background by hoping it would stay there but instead it came steadily forward out of the background and into clear light.

"Halooo!" said Mike the Apron. It was so loud in the hall we could pretend not to hear what he was saying. I pretended. He leaned forward and said more loudly, "Hello."

Martine looked at him with her eye.

"My name's Mike," he said.

But she didn't say anything.

"Your buddy Todd and me are friends," he said.

"Hello," she said tiredly.

"You close to a bingo, guy?" he said to me and came around so that he was looking over my shoulder and I felt the warm arm of his breath fall on my neck.

Then he crouched down so that he was the same level as me and into my ear he said, "You go, tiger."

After that he stood back up, slapped me on the back which I hate and shouted, "Later, you two!" He shaped his mouth to say the word "baaa" but he might have only been burping. With a wink, he walked away.

We continued playing for a while without saying anything. From the high ceiling a strong light fell over the woman onstage who continued to turn the big wire basket. People kept yelling. Others slept. I know it's un-Christian to feel this way, but the thought that Martine didn't especially want to talk to Mike made me very happy. And for that and several other reasons I stayed happy for the rest of the night and went to bed happy and woke up happy too.

SIXTEEN

A FEW DAYS LATER I SAW GRETA DEANE AS I WAS coming home from work at the woodshop. I'd taken a shortcut across some fields and I saw her standing near the cows that she likes so much and spends time with. Payton has a small dairy farm but I never go work there because staff knows I'm mostly afraid of animals. I heard Raykene once describe Greta as one of "God's elect, as pure as rainwater." The cows were on the other side of the fence from Greta and as I got closer I saw that she was talking to them. I came up alongside her and stood there.

"Hi, Todd," she said, and then she pointed to a cow and in her voice that always went up at the end she said, "That's Eveline?"

"Hi," I said. Because of Martine I'd begun looking at girls more carefully and I saw that Greta seemed different. She was wearing green stones in her earlobes and painted swirls around her eyes and the black wing of hair that cut across her forehead was polished shiny. Eveline the cow meanwhile stood looking at us. Her jaw went regularly around in circles and stuff fell silently from her butt.

"What's up?" Greta said.

"Nothing special," I said and then I suddenly added, "I was with Mike on Lawn Crew when he went to your house!"

Greta smiled at me happily and said, "Did you know Eveline was pregnant last year? She gave birth to a calf named Ezekiel?"

"Pregnant," I said.

"She told me it was a hard delivery?" Greta said. "But she was very happy to have her baby?"

"She told you that?"

"Yes."

"Mike said he was helping you with something."

"Cows," she said, "are sensitive to heat?"

"He said he might have to see you again."

"But they don't sweat or even pant like dogs with their tongues out and they can only get rid of body heat by breathing?"

"What?" I said.

"Did you know that?" she asked.

I looked at her.

"Um, no," I said.

"Gotta go." She turned around to leave.

Greta Deane never said goodbye. I remembered that. I watched her walk away in her tall body that slowly got smaller in the distance and I wondered exactly which meds she was taking. Ever since I'd had the conversation with Martine I've been thinking lots about meds. I've been remembering something I forgot which was that in Six Winds I had a staff named Prashad who had a ponytail and called meds "potions." He said he'd tried them all because he was curious. He said, "Todd, the human brain is a chemical factory and I believe in full employment."

Prashad told me that he liked to imagine what the inventor of the specific medication looked like, based on the effects it had on him. He was sure that Valium was designed by somebody pale and quiet, who lived near the ocean and turned the calming noise of the sea into a pill that made the same thing happen to a living person. Ritalin was probably invented by a lady with buck teeth and frizzy hair. But Risperdal, he said, was clearly made by someone who was very fat and slow and liked nothing better than lying in bed while feeling the gigantic downward pressure of a weight on his head.

I turned to go, pressing my feet into the grass as I went home. Risperdal was one of several pills Martine took but it was the Risperdal that was crushing her head with its weight just like I was crushing the grass under my feet, smash. Scientists don't even know exactly why Risperdal works but they know it crushes heads wonderfully. Mr B says that it was discovered in 1953 in the European country of Belgium. He says it's what they call a *dopamine antagonist*. Dopamine is the gasoline your brain nerves run on and Risperdal eats this gasoline which means your brain moves slower when you take it. You shout less. You feel like you're sitting underwater in a chair while breathing comfortably.

Martine was taking a four-milligram Orally Disintegrating Tablet of Risperdal every morning and night. The pill came in a color called "coral" and was kept along with other pills in a locked cabinet in the Med Center. Because Martine was a newbie, she didn't have her pills sealed into a long roll of plastic like I did. Instead, every morning the psychiatric social worker or the nurse brought them to her and watched her take them. They had done this to me too for several years before they'd finally trusted me to take them on my own.

I left the fields and cut across the large lawn and then home.

As I entered the cottage Tommy Doon looked up from the television and said, "It's her, isn't it?"

"No, it's not," I said.

"You didn't say 'who' and that means I caught you," he said and laughed out loud.

I struggled not to slam the door of my bedroom. Did he mean Martine? Did he mean Greta Deane? Who did he mean? A part of me was continuing to fill up with a kind of hate for Tommy Doon that made me want to do something bad. Instead of doing anything I took my meds and then listened to Englebert Humperdinck for several hours. I made dinner alone and fell asleep.

The next morning Tommy Doon wasn't up yet when I made breakfast and I was still thinking about Greta Deane with the sliding voice and Martine who was crushed by pills. I slowly pulled my meds out and looked at them with a new curiosity as they sat in their little puffy clear compartments. They were given to me to "make you feel like yourself." They were "part of your commitment to being the best villager you can be." These were MY meds, alone in the whole world. They had my name on them in small typed letters. It was the Law that I take all of them and I did just that, swallowing them with a glass of water as usual and heading out the front door.

That morning I was going to the Demont cafeteria to work. As I walked towards the van I was surprised to see that Mike the Apron was at the wheel. That was strange because normally a staff named Heidi drives. The other thing that was strange was that there were already six people in the van and one of them was Martine, who was staring straight ahead like she didn't see me. I stopped at the entrance to the van, uncertain what to do.

"That's right," Mike said. He was wearing big mirrored sunglasses that made him look like a fly. "In you go," he said, smiling.

The only seat available was next to Martine. I took it. Mike slowly backed the van out of the parking space and then began driving forward as Martine sat on the bench next to me, saying nothing.

"Hi," I said, but she made no response.

"Hi," I said again, and this time she nodded just a tiny bit.

Meanwhile, we continued moving down the road. Mike was chatting with the girl in the front seat whose name was Clarissa. She was from England. She spoke in an English way. Normally I don't pay much attention to what's outside the windows because I've taken this drive ten thousand times, but having Martine seated next to me made me hugely interested in everything that was happening in the gas stations, pizzerias, tire stores, factory outlets, Chinese restaurants, rug showrooms and mini-markets we passed. Every person I saw out the window seemed to be waiting for something. I hadn't noticed this before. I hadn't noticed before how the clouds were suspended in the sky like fruit in Jell-O. I hadn't noticed how everywhere I turned things were getting ready to jump forward and become something else. Out of the corner of my eye I could see Martine's profile cutting the scenery like the prow of a boat.

"Um," I said softly, so that Mike couldn't hear, "how are you?"

"The walls have ears," she said, also softly, staring straight ahead.

"Dudes, everything okay back there?" Mike said to his windshield.

"Okay," I said loudly as the van slowly rounded a turn and the tan brick buildings of the high school came into view. Immediately afterwards Mike pulled into the parking spot. When he turned off the car, he picked up a clipboard with a piece of paper on it.

"Okay, let's see," he said. "Higgins and Jones and Kosciuski to Custodial, Meyers and Bell to Physical Plant. Oh, and Martine and Todd, you wait here."

The other people got slowly out of the van. When they were all out and walking on the paths towards the high school, Mike turned to us and smiled his special fake smile.

"Hello, guys," he said.

Neither of us said anything.

"So are you wondering"—he looked at us while slowly bringing his two index fingers together and touching them—"why this for you two today?"

Still neither of us said anything. But Mike didn't seem to care. He said, "I thought that since you both are buddies and this is Martine's first day on the job, she should work alongside you, Todd. That okay?"

"Yes," I said.

Mike grinned which was like a smile but smaller. "Somehow I had the feeling it would be. You'll be in the cafeteria kitchen today. So, off you go."

Martine stepped out of the van first. I was about to follow her, when Mike shot his arm out and touched my forearm, which I don't like.

"Friends looking out for friends, if you know what I'm saying." He pulled down his mirrored sunglasses and looked at me. The whites of his eyes were filled with exploded red lines. "Nothing's free, bud. Remember that. Including introductions to new arrivals."

"Okay."

I got out of the van and led Martine silently along the waving concrete path towards the heavy main door of the school. Soon we were walking down the corridors that were filled with glass cases of trophies and streaming blue and red ribbons. It was early in the day and the students rushed by us to get to classes. They made a roar like an indoor swimming pool. They were small but they dressed like adults. The girls wore lipstick and painted eyes. The boys had hats. On the wall the theme of the Fall Festival was *Africa!* Paper cutouts of animals lined the hallway. A hyena walked with a lion. A giraffe went upwards so that its neck bent at ninety degrees where the ceiling began.

Mostly the students didn't look at us because they were used to us. Versions of us had been coming here from Payton Living-Center for many years. As we walked Martine turned towards me and said:

"Not only do the walls have ears—"

"What?" I said.

"They have eyes and noses!"

"What?" I said again.

She smiled and said, "Tereze has been giving me the beam."

"Um," I said.

"I mean watching me when I take my pills. Like a hawk. But it's too late because I'm already off the Rasperdoll."

She stopped what she was doing which was turning a corner and looked at me with the eye which was open especially wide.

"You get me?"

"Yes, I do."

"You want in? I can show you how."

Did I want in? Did I want to stop taking the drug that was making me feel like I was being personally pulled to the ground by someone and was always asleep in my body? The problem as usual was the Law. It leaned against you like a tall building of rules. It could fall on you at any moment.

"I don't know," I said.

She made a face and started walking again.

We got to the end of the hall and entered the swinging metal doors of the kitchen. I pushed forward and when the door opened the first thing I saw was Louise across the room mixing something in a big aluminum bowl. She looked up and a smile came across her face and she said:

"Hey, you!"

Louise was a big roundish woman with short gray hair who had worked in the kitchen of Demont for many years. After my first week there she had said, "You ever got any problem with anybody out there in the cafeteria, you just send them to me." Then she hooked her thumb towards her chest.

"Who's your girlfriend?" she now asked.

"This is Martine."

"Well, hi, Martine. You look like a secret agent or something with that eye of yours. But I bet you been told that a hundred times."

Martine stared at the floor.

"Not too talkative, I see, but that's okay, as long as you know how to chop."

Martine still said nothing.

"You guys got a big pile of potatoes to get through, and carrots too. Todd, I'll let you show Miss Martine the ropes, if you don't mind."

"That's fine."

Martine stood there, not moving and staring at the floor.

"Come with me," I said, and took her to the clothes closet in a smaller room off the cafeteria kitchen that had some lockers in it and a shower. I liked that she didn't know what to do and I did.

"These are the aprons!" I said loudly, and while she was looking at them I said in a less loud voice, "Maybe I can think about it."

"What?"

"Stopping taking the Risperdal."

"Good. Do you wanna know how to fake taking them?"

"Maybe."

My feelings pushed out of me towards Martine as strongly as the Law pushed back.

"Double good," she said. "We'll meet later and I'll show you what to do."

I was so happy at the idea of meeting her later that I closed my eyes without knowing it.

"Now put the apron on me," she said. When I opened my eyes again I saw that she'd stuck her hands straight up in the air like someone surrendering in a war and was waiting and smiling.

"Okay," I said, in a soft voice that sounded strange to me. I hooked the strings around her hands and then let the whole thing settle over her like a snowfall that went easily down over her body even though it was suddenly being blown sideways by a hard, invisible gust of wind.

SEVENTEEN

MY BROTHER CALLED FOR HIS WEEKLY CALL last night, and wanted to talk about how "stressed out" he was at work, but I wanted to talk about my Idea. I wanted to talk about coming home for an extended visit that maybe turned into forever and, as part of that, bringing Martine with me. I was now thinking about Martine constantly. But before I could talk about any of it, my brother said, "Oh, and how's it going with the new guy?"

"Which guy?"

"Mike, you said his name was?"

I could hear his sons yelling in the background.

"I know," he said, "I was supposed to call your people about him but I haven't gotten around to it yet. But that's 'cause I've been crazy busy with this huge impact study. Plus, I was thinking, Toddster, that your stuff would blow over soon. It usually does. So did it?"

"Nate?"

"Yes?"

"Can I come home?"

"Ah, Christ," my brother said quietly after a pause.

"What?" I asked.

"Again? I mean, really, after everything we've talked about?"

"But I wanna come home."

"I know you do." He took a long drink that filled the phone with clinking ice. "My knowing isn't the problem. The problem is that you wake up every day and you think, *What can the world do for me today?* That's the problem. But the world is full of people jammed with stuff to do in their lives, Tubes, stuff that is incredibly busy and important to their families, even if it doesn't seem real to you. The question is, why am I even telling you this?"

"So when *can* I come home?"

"My point, exactly."

"Soon?" I said.

My brother sighed. "You're in the very best place in the world for you. You know that Mom busted her butt to get you there. That's the first thing to remember. The second thing is do *not* fuck it up, okay?"

Sometimes after he would spray my dingus with hair spray he'd stand around watching with his friends as the heat of the burning made me cry from the pain. They'd be laughing until I started crying. Then they'd stop laughing and look at me in surprise.

Now he sighed again into the phone and in a different, happier tone of voice, he said, "God, I love the dusk. Remember how we used to sit on the back deck when we were kids just before supper, with the light changing in the backyard and the darkness kinda coming out of the woods and everything getting all spooky and mysterious for a few minutes? I think if I was a poet I'd have written about it."

"No," I said.

He never got punished for hurting me, not once. Not when he put rocks in my bed or teased me till I got volts. Not when he did a wedgie and pulled my underwear till it hurt or once swung a bat and cracked me with it in the head at the Goldsteins' Fourth of July picnic. Nothing ever happened to him except that he stayed and I left. Small, chunky sounds came out of the phone. He was chewing ice. "How about," he said, "the way Dad in the warm months would pour himself a stiff one and head out to the deck of the house, like clockwork, every day at six, and never miss a day?"

"Um," I said.

"God, he loved that backyard deck!"

"The deck," I said.

The deck was attached to the house. The house was in the town of Grable where we lived, on top of a hill that looked out on other houses sitting repeatingly on shelves in the same hill below us.

"That deck," my brother said, "was his own little piece of paradise."

"Right," I said. I was getting ready to ask him about coming home again. I had to ask him. It was important that I ask him. The problem would be the "incident." I knew it would. Maybe it was time to think again about the "incident." Maybe it was time to think about it again from beginning to end. According to Nate the incident had changed everything. The incident had happened when Nate, Beth and the kids had flown out to

Payton for the very first time to see me, just before our parents began to die.

"I miss him so much," he said softly.

"I know," I said into the phone while I watched him and his wife walk towards me out of memory that day, crossing the Payton lawn to my cottage. Behind them ran two little boys who were fighting loudly. I had never met his wife before then. She was tall and thin and wore a long dress that hung straight down from her shoulders like clothes off a hanger. From that dress a thin arm shot out. I shook it.

"Hello, Beth," I said to her.

"Hi!" she said loudly, and then I shook the tiny hands of his two sons. After that we got into the car and drove directly to a restaurant about ten minutes from Payton called Bob's Cabin. This was a big modern restaurant built onto the original old tiny cabin that once held miners. On the day we went there it was filled mainly with old people eating quietly. We sat down and I quickly ordered the special of the day which was the fried chicken platter. But first I made sure there was no peanut oil used in the frying by asking the waitress. I'm allergic not only to sesame seeds but also to nuts which if I eat them can cause someone to have to stab me with an EpiPen to keep me from going into anaphylactic shock that closes the throat.

"Nate was right," Beth said, nodding after the waitress left, "you run a pretty tight ship, Todd."

"Thank you," I said.

After that Beth kept trying to look into my eyes while she talked which I don't like. She was moving her mouth a lot but she was down the table from me and her voice kept getting a little bit lost in the restaurant sounds. I watched and listened and after a while it became clear that she was talking about her children. She was saying they had incredible appetites. She was saying they were talented at tai chi and soccer and math and painting and that their teachers loved them.

"Four gold stars in a row had never happened before," Beth was saying when a waiter brought our food and I stopped trying to listen and started eating. The name of my platter was the Cluck Tower. It had many pieces of chicken piled on a dome of french fries. At a certain point during the meal my brother left the table to go to the bathroom and Beth leaned forward and said, "You gotta forgive us for talking your ear off today, Todd. It's just excitement, is what it is. Nate is so proud of what you've accomplished and it means a lot to him to have you here. You know what? It means a lot to me too. Family is family, right?"

"Family," I said.

"I'm curious," she said quickly, "about your downtime at your, you know, place you're at. So, like, what do you do when you're not working?"

"I listen to records," I said.

"Records?" she said and clapped her hands together. "God, I haven't heard that term for years. Do you have a turntable? Or do you mean CDs?"

"And sometimes the oldies station," I said.

Her cell phone rang. The reason I know is because she made a face and began digging in her purse. We had been sitting at the restaurant table so long that many of the old people had left and younger people had replaced them and the noise of talking had become much louder. I hadn't heard the ringing over the sound.

Beth glanced at her phone and said, "This is a very important call." Then she stared at me for a short moment like she was trying to see something in my eyes.

"Todd, can I count on you for just one second," she said, "to keep an eye on the boys? I'll be literally less than a minute. I wouldn't ask, but it's a business call I've been waiting for all week. All I need is one minute, okay?"

Beth would later say that I said, "Yes." But all I really said was, "What?"

She held the cell phone to her ear and got up from the table and walked fast away from the loud dining room while holding an arm out in the air in front of her to hear better.

"My God, really?" I heard her yell as she left the room.

I continued eating my fried chicken. The boys were named Steven and Cam. They were eight and seven. Steven, the older one, was trying to teach Cam that you could shoot the paper end of a straw by blowing into it. I finished two chicken drumsticks fast and then turned my attention to the fries. They were crisp but still hot and floury inside, just the way I liked them. Suddenly a loud noise came through the air and I looked up.

Out the window I could see that the boys had run onto Eagle Avenue. I could also see that a car had swerved to avoid them and smashed into another car that was parked along the curb. A large cloud of steam rushed into the air above one of the cars.

I returned to eating the french fries in a special way where I first nibbled the crusts off and then mashed the rest of the softer parts into a paste.

A burst of shouting from outside the window made me look up again. The steam had cleared and the boys were still standing on the street while people ran towards them from every direction. One of the boys had something on his face. Suddenly Beth appeared in the window. She was also running. I reached for the ketchup and squirted it on my plate. I love to blend the potatoes and ketchup together and I was doing that when I heard Beth again, but now much more loudly. She was no longer outside but back at the entrance to the dining room. There were stains on her white shirt. Her mouth was open and her chest was heaving like she was trying to breathe. Finally she got her breath and when she did she began to scream.

The screaming caused other people who were eating to stop with their forks and knives in the air. As the screaming went on my brother ran into the dining room carrying Cam in his arms while Steven ran behind him holding his pants leg and looking scared. Cam's face was striped with blood and he was screaming like his mother, but higher. My brother's eyes were very wide and in a loud, strange voice he yelled to the whole room, "He was cut by flying glass but everything is okay!"

Beth's screaming had just been sounds but now it became words as she faced me. The first word was, "What!" This was followed by, "The fuck is wrong with you?"

Her arm was pointing at me and her chest was still heaving. I had been holding my spoon of potato-and-ketchup paste in the air while she yelled. When she stopped yelling I put it in my mouth.

"That's just not right," I heard a woman say.

My brother announced to the restaurant, "So sorry for the intrusion, folks. The EMT has been called. Please return to your meals." Then to Beth in a lower, more normal voice he said, "I'll say it again. You left *him* in charge?"

"Me?" yelled Beth loudly. "Now you're blaming me?"

No one had returned to eating. In fact the whole room had become completely quiet to watch better.

"I'm not blaming anybody," my brother said. "But come on, Beth."

"I was gone less than three minutes, for god's sake!" she shouted.

My brother looked down at Cam who was crying but more

softly and said, "I know it stings, sweetie, but we'll get you fixed up in a jiffy."

"Give him to me now, goddammit!" Beth screamed.

But Nate continued to look down at Cam and whisper things to him while ignoring her. Then Steven left Nate and went running towards Beth who started screaming again just as sirens suddenly got loud outside the restaurant and the doors flew open and burly ambulance-men came rushing into the room.

Later that day, my brother drove me back to Payton to drop me off instead of having me stay with them at their hotel for the long weekend as we'd planned. He said, "I know you didn't mean anything. Beth just shouldn't have left you in charge. Believe me when I tell ya it's nobody's fault, but . . ."

Then my brother didn't say anything for a little while. When he started talking again he told me Cam would probably be fine and both he and his wife hoped there wouldn't be scars but they were cutting their trip short and leaving that day. Also, I might not be coming back home as we'd planned for the future and he hoped I understood. He said he really hoped that I understood. He said he thought there was "a lesson here for everybody involved." He knew that I had a "good soul, the Aaron family unit," and he was almost positive that everything would "eventually blow over."

But all that was several years ago and I'd never gone home or seen his wife and children again and in the meantime I was still on the phone with my brother on the same call where he'd been talking about our Dad. It was a long call and he'd been drinking steadily and he was now very drunk. I could hear he was very drunk because he had the same falling-loose voice Daddy did when he'd been drinking. "Tubes," he said, "all I ever wanted was for you to be safe and happy. Mom made me swear to look after you when she was gone, did you know that?

Cried in my arms over it, actually, and she was a tough old girl. Well, I have."

"Have what?"

"Taken care of you."

"Okay," I said, "but Nate?"

"Don't ask."

"When can I come—"

"Enough!"

There was a silence during which I heard the ice cubes clinking as he drank. In a low voice like he was talking partly to himself he said, "Just 'cause you're sick doesn't mean you can't also be selfish as hell." He made a sound in his chest that wasn't a word.

"But Nate?" I repeated.

"What, Todd?" he yelled. I could hear him breathing heavy on the phone.

"After Bob's Cabin you said I could come home one day."

"Ah, fuck."

"Nate?" I said.

There was a silence.

"Nate?" I said again. But the phone coughed in my ear and spit out a hiss and I realized that my brother had hung up.

EIGHTEEN

MARTINE AND I MET FOR ME TO LEARN HOW NOT to take my meds under a large tree the villagers called Mr. Breeze. It was called that because it was alone on the lawn and whenever the wind blew it made a special rushing sound of air through the leaves. I was excited as I watched her come towards me with her back hunched and her head fallen forward. Soon she was under Mr. Breeze where no one could hear us. Maybe no one could see us either. The branches came out of the trunk and lowered thickly around us. She stood up straight and smiled.

"Hi!" she said

"Hello, Martine."

"It's already working!" she said.

I looked at her. "What is?"

"My not taking the pills."

"How do you know?"

"Can't you tell?"

"No."

"Let's sit down."

"Okay," I said, and the two of us sat down at exactly the same time. Martine laughed.

"Would you like to see my dead eye?" she asked.

"Your dead eye?"

I looked around through the hanging branches. I could see that no one anywhere was coming towards us from any direction and that we were alone.

"Sure," I said.

"I don't usually do this," she said.

"No."

"But you're a pal."

"Thank you."

"Or something. Come closer."

Her eyepatch was very dark and covered a big part of her face. I'd wondered what was behind it before, and whether there was a black hole that you could see her brain through, or a bunch of veins, or did she use it like a wallet in her head where she kept keys or coins. Using my hands I pushed myself closer until our knees were almost touching. I'd never been this close to her before. Light, interrupted by leaves, fell all over us. The wind breathed quietly. Liquid was pouring into my mouth from places inside my throat when, "Here," she said, and slipped the entire eyepatch off her head. Where the clear pond of the eye would normally be there was a milky blue thing that bulged in the socket.

"This is it," she said.

Maybe it looked like an agate or a stone. Maybe it was like she was wearing a rock in her head.

"Wow," I said, "that's your eye."

"It *was* my eye. Now it's just a shell. After it healed we decided to keep it there rather than put a glass one in."

"Your eye," I said again, because I didn't know what to say.

"My eye," she said.

"Hunh."

"Now show me something of yours," she said.

"Like what?"

"I don't know. Something to match."

"I don't have anything like that."

"I bet you do. What part of you don't you like?"

I didn't know what she was talking about but what I did know was that she was very close to me, under the tree with the stuck-out branches. Also I knew that everything was slowing down and then slowing down further. Usually I felt a kind of fatigue all the time because of the Risperdal but I didn't feel that just now. It was warm out. Sweat was coming onto my skin. I could feel it running down my forehead. But her forehead was dry.

"Show me," she said, but not in a harsh way like she sometimes spoke.

As I thought of what I could show her I continued looking at her face. Without the eyepatch on it was now a regular face except one of the eyes was clouded. I noticed that when she moved the one normal eye the cloudy eye moved also. It was like having two people in one head.

"I like you," I said. I couldn't remember ever saying that to a girl or if I did it was many years ago. Usually, I only said it to staff.

"I know," she said. "So, what part don't you like? Your gut?"

I didn't mind my gut. I didn't mind that I sometimes breathed so much through my mouth that little scabs formed on my lips. I didn't mind that I shaved badly and left patches of sprouted hair on my face or that I sometimes smelled from various parts of myself. I didn't mind at all. I still didn't understand her question.

"I told my parents about you," she said.

I was so close to her that I could see the tiny, individually alive silver hairs on the skin of her face.

"Your parents?" I said.

"I said you were a new friend, and very nice, and smarter than you seemed." She laughed.

"Thank you."

"Todd, do you want to touch it?"

"What?"

"My eye."

"Your eye?"

"Yes."

"I don't know."

"The nerves in it are dead and I can't feel anything. You can touch it, as long as your hands are clean. Are your hands clean, Todd?"

I'm what Raykene and other staff call a "real stickler" for cleanliness. I wash my hands several times a day.

"Yes," I said.

"Go ahead."

So under the big branchy tree I reached forward very slowly and holding out my finger I touched her naked eye. It was warm and slightly sticky. It felt like the inside of a body that happened to be in your face.

"Martine," I said.

"My eye," she said.

"Your eye," I said slowly, "is warm."

"Well, duh."

Then we stayed under the tree silent for a little bit while the breeze picked up. After a while I thought I heard the humming of insects, but it was Martine's voice. She was talking. I realized that in the meantime I'd forgotten where I was. I was a little disappointed to remember. But she was talking about the pills. She was saying that it was actually easy. She was saying that whenever they checked on you about taking the meds you had to first distract them by telling a joke or asking a serious question.

"Then you palm the pill like this," she said, and placed a pill she'd brought in the little fold of flesh between her thumb and index finger. She put the palm to her mouth.

"Gug," she said. "You actually say the word 'gug.'"

"Okay."

"It sounds like swallowing. And remember the joke."

"Right."

"Do you know any jokes?"

"No."

"I'll teach you one."

"Thank you, Martine."

Not taking my pills meant something so bad would happen to me that I'd never let myself even think about it. But it was exciting to be this close to Martine under Mr. Breeze. She was like the princess out of the giant book of fairy tales my Momma read me who could change crawling animals into pretty winged birds with a snap of her fingers and make people fall asleep while talking out loud. The wind in my pants rose upwards into my head.

"I like you," I said again.

"I can tell," she said and winked at me with the good eye.

NINETEEN

LOVE WAS INVENTED IN 1177. A MAN NAMED Chrétien de Troyes discovered it. According to Mr. B, he felt something that he hadn't felt before and he looked at what it was that caused that feeling and he realized it was a girl. She was sitting on a rock near him and he was looking at her from his horse. A lot of people rode horses at this time. Chrétien was so surprised at his feelings that he wrote a very long poem about them. This poem became very famous. In the poem he was named Lancelot and the girl he loved was named Queen Guinevere. Chrétien used very fancy language when talking about how he felt about Guinevere. Now we describe these feelings differently. Mr. C says that some of the ways to describe a person in love today are:

1. *emotionally inebriated*
2. *endorphin-flooded*
3. *inexplicably buoyant*
4. *erotically fixated*

In 1177 Lancelot thought the sun was always shining on Guinevere. He thought she was as pure as the snow. He thought she was a perfect person. He thought that maybe there had never been anyone more perfect than her before in the history of the world.

Lancelot actually believed this.

That was love.

After seeing Martine under Mr. Breeze and touching her sticky eye with a finger I stayed awake one whole night and day thinking about her. Then I almost cut myself very badly the next afternoon at the Demont High School cafeteria from being tired. When I finally did fall asleep that second night, the first thing I did when I woke up the next morning was to remember Martine's instructions to stop taking my Risperdal. I had taken it for so many days in a row that it wasn't easy to stop. I kept starting to take it several times before I finally flushed it down the toilet. I hadn't seen Martine since our time under the tree but as I watched the little pill go down into the swirling water of the toilet I thought of her. I also began immediately to feel anxious.

Later that same morning I was given a work assignment to do with Mike. My vocational manager Dave told me that Mike had requested it. He explained that our job would be a walkaround of the property line of Payton to make sure the fence was mended. We'd carry twists of metal that we could use to patch the fence and bolt cutters and pliers and also red flags that we'd place if there was a hole too big to fix. Then a crew would come by with power tools later on and whole pieces of fencing and cover the hole. He sent me out to meet Mike and as I came up to him Mike looked at me.

"So, sport," he said.

I didn't say anything.

"How's it going?" he asked.

"Fine."

We walked across a lawn together and he pointed to a hole in the fence. "Take this patch here and hold it over the hole while I twist the wire."

I did.

"Anything you wanna tell me?" he asked.

"Um."

"About your girl, for example."

"My girl?"

"I told you before, don't pretend. How's it going with one-eye?"

"Martine," I said.

"Yes."

"I like her," I said loudly.

"Congratulations."

"She showed me her eye!" I said.

Mike gave one of his coyote-chuckles. "Keep it down," he said. "I can tell you're excited."

There was a silence. It had been several hours since I'd skipped taking Risperdal and I began to feel something. It was a cramp in my stomach like from eating rotten food. We worked on the fence.

"What else she show you?" he asked.

"Just her eye."

Mike snorted. "Please. I've seen her file. Here's something you didn't know. Our little Miss Martine was thrown out of a place for what they're callin' "inappropriate social conduct." That's code, guy. It means hanky-panky, if you catch my drift. You picked one helluva live wire."

Then he bent down and began fitting the mesh screen over the fence. I was holding the pliers in my hand while I looked at all the open flesh at the back of his neck.

"But I'm sure she's been saving something just for you," he said to the fence.

From the very beginning there was a certain way that people would speak where I didn't understand what they said but I could feel its meaning against the skin of my body. They usually did this while smiling. Momma always said they "underestimated" me. They looked at the expression on my face which was often hung up on one side like I was tasting something funny and they talked around me. They talked at me. They threw words at me like I was the wall of a barn. They thought I didn't understand but sometimes I did.

Now I gripped the pliers as hard as I could in my hand.

"And I bet she's got some real bounce in them britches of hers, if you get me," he said.

I gripped harder. A red, straining line slowly connected my clenching jaws and the bones of my squeezing hand.

Mike turned smiling and put his gloved hands up on either side of his face.

"But hey," he said, "it ain't none of my business, really. I just like joshing you, okay?"

I relaxed my grip on the pliers.

"Okay."

We kept working as the cramp in my stomach got steadily worse. Soon I thought I might have to throw up from the cramp. We finished the work and as we were getting ready to go, Mike said, "Well done. And I'd like your help again."

"My help," I said. But I couldn't hear what he was saying too well. A few minutes earlier a strange ringing sound had begun in my head.

"Peace Cottage tomorrow in the afternoon, you free?"

"I don't know."

"Todd, it's an important tutoring session and I promised I'd be there for it. I'll recon with you tomorrow and check in," he said. At least I think that's what he said because the sound was getting even louder, gradually. Mike the Apron fist-bumped me goodbye, and I walked back to the cottage. It didn't occur to me that the sound was in some way from not taking the Risperdal after having taken it every day for 4,466 days. The sound was accompanied by an anxiety over the sound and I wondered if the sound was maybe the noise of anxiety itself, getting worse.

When I opened the front door of the cottage, the first thing I saw was Raykene sitting on the couch with Tommy Doon sitting next to her watching television with the sound turned off. Raykene is usually smiling and even when she's not smiling her eyes and cheeks and mouth are still drawn up from all the smiling that's gone through her face. But this time she was looking at me with a very serious expression. I wasn't sure I'd ever seen her make that expression before.

"Todd," she said.

"Hello, Raykene."

"We need to talk."

"Talk?"

"In private," she said. "You mind if we have a little chat in your room?"

When we entered my room she shut the door behind us. The volume of the TV went back on in the living room and immediately we heard gunshots and sounds of people yelling. She asked me to sit down on my desk chair and stood standing in the room with her hands on her hips.

"We've got a situation," she said.

"We do?"

"Right now, before you do anything else, I need you to tell me everything you know about Mike Hinton."

TWENTY

GRETA DEANE HAD TRIED TO KILL HERSELF with pills. That's what Raykene told me as she stood in front of me in my bedroom. She was now in the hospital and she was almost dead, Raykene said. It had just happened and no one knew about it yet. But a maintenance worker had recently seen Mike the Apron enter Peace Cottage, "looking sneaky," and that's why she was here, Raykene said. No one had specifically asked her to come see me, but she was "following out every possible crazy lead."

"'Crazy lead,'" I repeated.

"You know, hunch, idea, whatever. I'm just trying to put things together here."

"Right," I said.

"Todd?"

"What?"

"Are you sure you're okay, honey? You look a little green

around the edges. Straight up—something wrong? I've known you long enough to know."

"I have to go to the bathroom," I said.

"Well, you go right ahead, sugar. I'll wait."

I walked out and into the bathroom where I threw up very hard. The noise of the television was so loud no one heard me. I washed my face and drank some water from the tap and when I got back to my room Raykene was sitting on my bed. She got up as I entered.

"Better, my friend?" she said.

"Yes."

"Good. So what I was saying was that I don't wanna make you feel bad about telling on a buddy who probably has nothing to do with this anyway, but I'm just checking everything out because this could be a huge problem for Payton. We're talking *huge*, Todd."

I didn't say anything. I just stared at her. Often, it's easier not to speak. Also my balance was suddenly off and I felt like maybe I was too tall and so sat down on the bed.

"You're looking a little shook up by this," she said and studied me with her eyes, "and who can blame you? So let's make it easy. I'm just gonna run some questions by you and you nod your head yes or no, okay?"

I still didn't say anything.

"Over the last few weeks you spent several afternoons with Mike."

I nodded yes.

"You went to Peace with him."

I shook my head no.

"No?"

"No, I stayed behind."

"But he said he was going there?"

"Yes, but I didn't see him go."

"Fine, but remember you can just nod if it's easier. Okay, now the important part. When he went there, did he say exactly why he was—"

But just then we felt the little vibration of the front door of the cottage opening and shutting. A moment later the volume of the TV was muted. Into the silence came the voice of Mike the Apron. It was high and excited.

"Is Todd in?" he asked.

"Todd Aaron and Raykene Smith," Tommy said loudly, "are in Todd Aaron's bedroom." Raykene looked at me and walked to the center of the room while holding her finger up to her mouth to shush me. We waited for a little bit but we didn't hear anything, not even the front door closing. Meanwhile I sat on the bed and rocked a little to distract myself from the nausea. The nausea was beginning again, along with the feeling that maybe one part of me was growing too hot and another too cold. This made me anxious and I tried to deep-breathe with my eyes closed like I'd been taught, to relax. When I opened my eyes Raykene had her hands on her hips and was looking at me carefully.

"Todd?" she said.

"Yes?"

"You look like you're about to hyperventilate. You worried about telling on a friend? I just stuck my head out and he's gone. No more questions for today, all right?"

"I'm okay."

"No, you're not," she said. "Come here, honey."

I got slowly up from the bed and went and stood in front of

her. She put her hands on my shoulders and said, "You know that none of this has got anything to do with you, you do know that, don't you?"

"I know," I replied.

"I wanna make sure you know," she said.

"I know."

"'Cause it doesn't. But what's strange is what just happened here with Mike at the door. That's weird." She stood there shaking her head. "That's not good."

I didn't say anything.

"Main thing is, I'm sorry you gotta deal with any of this. But I'm hoping it will all blow over soon. Okay?" I nodded yes and she grabbed me by the shoulders and squeezed them hard so that I could feel the rings on her fingers and then she left.

The strange feelings inside me continued going on for the rest of the afternoon. The ringing noise in my head got louder. I got even taller-feeling and also tried to vomit again but nothing came out and I just coughed on the toilet. Tommy Doon was watching me very carefully whenever I was in the living room and he turned the volume of the television up as far as it would go and sang along loudly with the commercials to try to rattle me. He was trying as hard as he could to give me volts but I ignored him. After dinner there was a special on the oldies radio station. Twice a week they play a Gold Block of songs from a group that goes on for more than an hour. This night it was the Beach Boys. I love the Beach Boys. Music from the radio is just air vibrating inside your ear but it throws moving pictures into your head that are almost as fun to watch and hear as real life. Plus, on this evening music made me forget about how bad I was feeling.

I had the volume on high in my earphones and I was listening to "Good Vibrations" when I saw the door of my room open fast. Tommy Doon was standing there, breathing heavy. I took the headphones off.

"You!" he shouted.

"What?"

"I've been yelling at you for five minutes that Mike Hinton is on the phone for you. It's urgent, jerk!"

"I'm sorry," I said, getting out of bed.

"No, you're not. You're a bad person and I know you're planning something."

"Planning something?" I stopped as I was walking out of the room.

"You have maps in your room and I think you're going to try to pull a caper with Mike Hinton and I'm going to tell on you."

Tommy Doon growled and clenched his jaws tight and shook his head like he was shivering and repeated loudly, "Tell on *you*!"

"Right," I said and walked past him to the phone on the wall.

"Hello?" I said.

"Where have you been?"

"Mike?"

"Why did I have to wait so long to talk to you?"

"What do you mean?"

"Cut the goofball bit. Were you talking to one of your girlfriends just now?"

"No."

"Someone from the administration?"

"No, I was listening to music."

"Well, listen to this, Mr. Popular, I'm in some deep shit but guess what, so are you."

The siren in my head had gone away while listening to the Beach Boys but now it started up again, along with the sick feelings. I wasn't certain what he was saying, so I did what I always did at times like this. I said the word, "Okay."

"Nothing's okay," said Mike. "Nothing in the whole fucking world is okay. Meet me at the hedge behind the woodshop tomorrow morning at seven o'clock sharp. Got it?"

That night was very bad. Every time as I was about to fall asleep I felt an electric shock that woke me back up. When I finally fell asleep I dreamed of a large mouth opening and shutting directly in front of my face. Then clouds blew quickly into the darkening sky while leaves wrinkled on all the trees in the forest and people came towards me out of the night with their teeth showing while they hissed like cats. I tossed in my bed for many hours and got the sheets wet from sweating. The next morning I was tired and very nervous. When I got outside to the hedge, Mike was already there and walking back and forth. Even though it was early in the day it was already hot out, with the sun pressing on you like an actual weight. He was wearing his white T-shirt and jeans.

"Anybody see you?" he asked as I came closer.

"I don't think so."

Mike lit a cigarette which I'd never seen him do before even though I always smelled them on his clothes and his breath.

"Okay, let's begin at the beginning. What do you know?" he said.

"About what?"

He made a groaning sound while smoke came from his nose.

"Do not," he said, "fuck with me today, as I'm not in the mood."

My mouth opened but no words came out.

"You know how serious this is," he said.

My mouth closed. "I'm not sure."

"What did you tell her?"

"Who?"

"Still pretending?"

"Still pretending what?"

"Lemme explain it to you, genius. Our futures, they're linked, see."

"Okay."

"Anything that happens to me, you were an accessory to it."

He shook another cigarette out of the pack and lit it with the one he'd been smoking.

"What'd you tell her?" he repeated. His eyes were small in his head.

"Who?"

Once I saw a man spun in something called a centrifuge. His face was pulled backwards into curved shapes from going fast. Mike made a centrifuge face. He seemed to be trembling with the strain of making the face. Then he stopped making it and looked at me.

"All I need out of you right now," he said slowly, "is to hear that you didn't tell Raykene Smith a single thing about us and Peace Cottage. Did you?"

I have never been able to lie. The main reason I know this is because people have always told me so. I said:

"She asked if you'd been there and I said yes."

He started to shout something and then stopped and instead of saying anything he took several big breaths of his cigarette while shutting his eyes. In a normal voice, after a little bit, he said:

"So she asked about me?"

"Yes."

"I see," he said calmly. Then he made another centrifuge face for a few seconds and shook a little again. Then he stopped making the face and smoked silently again for a few seconds.

"What did you tell her?"

"I told her I thought you went but I didn't know because I didn't see you."

"And then?"

"Then we heard you coming into my cottage and asking Tommy Doon where I was. Then we stopped talking and we didn't talk any more."

"So the two of you heard me walking in and asking for you?" His voice had now become almost pleasant. All the centrifuge-strain had gone completely away. This made me very relieved. I said happily, "Yes, that's right!"

Mike lifted his lips back off his yellow teeth, that were extremely long. They glistened with liquid. He blew air through them to make a strange hissing sound that frightened me. Then he turned around and began running away as fast as he could. The pointy cowboy boots made him bowlegged and as I watched he almost tripped and fell but he recovered his balance and kept on running.

TWENTY-ONE

THE SICKNESS GOT WORSE. I BEGAN TO SEE strange wavering edges around things that were often blue. Even if there was a green in front of me like the forest as I walked through it there was also blue on the sides of my eyes. To feel better I told myself that I was being "doughty" which means brave like Lancelot and that I was doing this because it would make Martine like me. But it was hard to work in the woodshop and even harder to work in the Demont High School cafeteria because I had to excuse myself often to go to the bathroom where I'd wash my hands and feel like I had to vomit even though I mostly couldn't. Raykene thought I was nervous about Mike the Apron and told the other staff to be extra-careful with me and "pamper" me whenever possible.

Lancelot had gotten his name because he'd fought many fights with his lance. My own lance was still lying in the woods where I'd left it and I began going out often in the mornings usually and touching the stick to remember that I was a person with a new Idea of going home to live with my family even if it hadn't happened yet. I was tired a lot but I still sometimes threw the stick-lance into trees as hard as I could. I liked throwing the lance. One morning when I returned from throwing it I saw a car parked in the driveway of the cottage. Inside the house I recognized Tommy's parents, who I'd met once before. They were very old and sitting at the kitchen table.

"Good morning, Todd," said Tommy's mother. "Out for a morning walk?"

"Good morning," I said.

"Agreed about the morning," said his father, "but the afternoon's gonna be a helluva thing."

"You mean hot, honey?" asked Mrs. Doon.

"Todd Aaron has got a secret plan to run away!" Tommy Doon said loudly. His mother looked at him. She had a big ball of hair on her head and a tiny triangular face and in the middle of that face was the red line of her lips. The lips opened.

"Tom-Toms, relax," she said.

"It's true!" he shouted angrily.

"Why so upset?" His father shrugged his shoulders. "It might be true, it might not be true. Big diff. He comes, he goes. He'll end up back here no matter what. 'Touch the earth and touch the sky,' right?"

The father looked at me. I was beginning to feel sick again and to try to feel better I began making my breakfast. I did this by removing the pouch of cereal from the cabinet, placing it in a bowl in the microwave and hitting the button across which a staff had taped the word "oatmeal." The oven coughed and began to breathe loudly.

"It's not true, is it," his father asked me, "about you running away on us?" He opened his mouth in laughter but no sound came out.

"No," I said. When the bell rang I took the bowl with the steaming pouch in it very carefully out of the microwave. Then I got a spoon and put everything on a plastic tray to carry it into my bedroom. There was a Barry Manilow Gold Block on the radio that morning and I wanted to listen to it while I ate.

"You see?" said the father. "So, just relax son, okay? Besides, why would anyone leave this place? It's a paradise. He's got all his needs taken care of, food, entertainment and, by the way, a very nice young man as a new roommate."

"Todd Aaron is ugly and he has a girlfriend!" Tommy Doon shouted. I ignored him and began slowly walking across the floor so I didn't drop the slippery plastic bowl off the tray like once happened and then I had to clean it up.

"You congratulating him, son?" said the father. "It sure sounds like that."

"Honey, please," said Mrs. Doon to her husband, "they said 'redirect' instead of 'engage,' remember?"

"Nooooo!" Tommy screamed. Then he started to cry. He was a fat bald person sitting in the chair in front of the television with the sound off and he was crying. His parents leaned towards him and each of them took hold of a different part of him while they yelled at each other in whispers. Tommy began to shout.

"He does have a girlfriend!" he yelled. "He has a girlfriend and it's not right!"

Back in my bedroom I turned on Barry Manilow as loud as I could. He was singing "Mandy." I started eating oatmeal and the sounds of Barry's voice mixed pleasantly with the faint screams of Tommy Doon and the taste of the oatmeal in my mouth and made me feel a little better. At a certain point there was a loud knocking on the door and because I wasn't using the headphones I could hear it. "Come in," I said.

Raykene opened the door.

"Is that who I think it is?" she asked, pointing to my radio. I turned it down.

"Maybe."

"Todd, honey, you crack me up. Listen, there's something important you should know which is that Mr. Rawson himself needs to talk to you. All right?"

"Yes."

Mr. Rawson was the head of Payton International. He was an important person who wore a shirt and tie and moved quickly and spoke with a warm, focused voice and remembered lots of little details about you. I sometimes saw him giving speeches in front of large crowds of people during the Christmas pageant and staff always pointed him out on TV, even though I almost never watched. He'd also known my Mom when she worked as the "parental liaison" a long time ago.

An hour later Raykene came by again and got me and brought me to the Main Hall where Mr. Rawson was waiting in an office. He looked very serious as we came in. He was wearing the box of a blue suit and sitting on one corner of his desk.

"Good morning to you, Todd," he said.

"Good morning, Mr. Rawson."

He studied me for a second. "You okay?"

"Yes."

"I might wish we were meeting under slightly more relaxed circumstances, but we're not in control of that, I'm afraid. We have some serious business to discuss today, and I'd like to start at the beginning if that's okay."

I said nothing.

"Tell me about your friendship with Mr. Hinton, or Mike, Todd. I know that things were a little rocky at the start."

Mr. Rawson had always spoken to me as if I was high-functioning, which I liked. I said:

"Mike frightened me because he looked like my father so much that when he sometimes talked I thought it was my Dad, who's dead."

Mr. Rawson nodded.

"Go on."

"And then we worked together and he told me he was my friend."

"Right," said Mr. Rawson. "And what happened more recently?"

"He said he had to go to Peace Cottage because he had some-one he was helping there."

Mr. Rawson looked at Raykene, who frowned and shook her head. He said to me pleasantly, "Just hold that thought one sec-ond, Todd, will ya?" Then from his pocket he took out a small radio. He put it on the table between us, and said, "Could you repeat that again, and pronounce clearly?"

"Yes," I said. "Mike said he had to leave the Lawn Crew while we were cutting grass and go to Peace Cottage because he had to help someone there. He said it was very important."

"I should note that we're talking to long-term resident Todd Aaron, and the date today is August third," said Mr. Rawson. "What did he ask you to do on these visits?"

"To continue working on the Lawn Crew by myself."

"Cutting grass?"

"No, raking."

"Did he ever say anything more specifically about what he was going to do at Peace Cottage?"

"I can't remember."

"You can't remember."

"No," I said.

"Todd, let me put it to you another way. Did you ever see what was going on inside, with this treatment he spoke of?"

"Um, no."

"I see. And is there anything else about Mike you'd like us to know?"

"I don't think so."

"Nothing at all?"

I thought for a second.

"He bought a toy."

Mr. Rawson looked confused. "A toy?"

"Yes, that he could fly."

"A toy plane?"

"Yes, that had a camera on it that he could fly around and see things with."

"Really?"

"He controlled it with a radio."

"And by camera—you mean like a video camera?"

"I think so."

"Dear Lord," said Raykene.

"He called it his eyes in the sky," I said.

Mr. Rawson's eyebrows mashed together in a single line. "Let me just get this straight, because it's important," he said slowly. "You're saying that Mike Hinton had a mobile video camera on a kind of radio-controlled plane or something?"

"Yes," I said.

Mr. Rawson shook his head and he and Raykene frowned at each other.

"And what was the last thing he said to you about Peace Cottage?" he asked.

"He said that the person he was helping there needed more tutoring."

"Tutoring?" Mr. Rawson and Raykene looked at each other. "That's the word he used?"

"I think so."

Mr. Rawson rubbed his eyes with a hand. He said, "I think that's enough for now. In the meantime, Todd, I need your word that if Mike Hinton tries to contact you in any way you'll tell us immediately. I'm giving you my personal cell phone number, Todd, which I never give anybody. That's how important this is, okay?"

"Yes."

Then they said some things quickly to each other and after that Mr. Rawson handed me a piece of paper with his cell phone number and thanked me a lot and said I might have to repeat what I'd said in front of some other people in the future. Raykene left to do something and he shook my hand again and told me that I looked a lot like my Momma.

"And your mother was important to us here, Todd," he said, "and made a difference in people's lives."

Momma worked in "food activism." She believed that nutrition was a "key overlooked sector" in the "institutional setting for the disabled." She wanted to improve menus by assigning all foods to one of three groups: green, red or purple so that every day each villager "ate a rainbow."

"Thank you," I said to Mr. Rawson.

"You're welcome," he said.

I said goodbye and left the office but when I began walking home I felt dizzy again and suddenly too tall and instead of going home I sat on a bench for a few minutes until I felt better. Then I decided to go into the woods to see the stick again. I didn't want to throw it, just see it and touch it and be back in the story of being a brave "old fox" with a secret plan to return home to his family. But when I parted the green pieces of the bushes what I saw made me very sad. The stick had been snapped in two. The wood where it was broken was still white and fresh which showed that someone had recently broken it and then put it back where it was.

For a moment I couldn't move but stayed perfectly still as the pain rose steadily upwards from my stomach and filled my eyes. When they spilled over, I began to cry.

I walked back home crying and was still crying as I opened the front door of the house and went inside. Tommy Doon was watching television and when he saw me he shouted happily:

"Todd Aaron crying! Todd Aaron crying!"

I went as fast as I could towards my room. I was just reaching the door when I heard him say loudly, "A note."

I turned.

"What?"

"A note, crybaby," he said again and made a pushing move with his chin. I saw an envelope sitting on a table.

"From who?" I asked.

"I don't know," said Tommy. "It was here when I got back." Then he slowly raised the volume of the television as loud as it would go while looking at me and smiling.

The note was in a regular envelope with my name written on it. I picked it up and took it into my room and opened it which meant tearing the envelope because it was sealed. Inside it was a piece of paper with words written on it. The words were these: "Eyes in the sky see EVERYTHING. We had an agreement and you broke your promise. Time to start looking over your shoulder."

I stared at the note and as I did I noticed that the letters were beginning to fade. I blinked to try to slow the fading down but they continued to grow dimmer and dimmer until finally the page was blank. I dropped the paper on the floor and stood very still in my room. More than anything else in the world at that moment I wanted to be away—away from coyote-people and schedules and the Day Program and most of all away from the campus of Payton LivingCenter. I wanted to travel through the air like a kite and land back in the crawl space beneath the kitchen stairs of my childhood house, crouching while people dropped their weight with thumps right above my head. I wanted to stand in the basement where the little windows crushed the light until it became so weak that you turned invisible.

Then Momma's voice came calling you upstairs for lamb chops and baked beans.

I stood there very still for another few minutes and then slowly I walked across the floor of the room until I got to the window. The glass of the window was warm with sunlight. I put my forehead against the warmth and looked out on the campus where people were walking and bending to tie their shoes and also making many small movements like clipping flowers or pulling out weeds or poking their hands into air as they had conversations with each other.

This wasn't my home. It pretended to be. It pretended with all its might that it was filled with people who were my family and also that it was the right place for me. But none of these things were true and they never would be. I wanted to take my

hand and shatter the window and the pretendingness into little bits. My real life was still going on somehow in the spaces of the house where I was born and the woods behind it. What I was seeing now out the window was a fake projection of a family like a movie on a sheet that they showed us once at a special needs summer camp.

Then the sheet was pulled away and we saw a couple of bored counselors sitting in the dark drinking beer.

PART

FOUR

TWENTY-TWO

E VER SINCE I HAD MY IDEA AND BOUGHT MAPS AT the mall I've been thinking about roads and also about what goes up and down roads which is mainly cars. Daddy loved cars and he bought new ones as much as possible. Cars were rooms with people in them that traveled fast and were called *Biscayne* and *Nova*, *Riviera* and *Corvair*, *Bonneville* and *Torino*. Their insides were of cool blue leather to sit in like swimming pools. They had panels of dangerous stalks and nobs on their dashboards and skins on their bodies painted fiery colors that made me afraid to touch them.

We took one to the beach once where my parents lay on the sand ignoring the folding waves and the sun and said to each other, "Isn't this lovely?" before they fell asleep. We drove one up into the cool air in the mountains to "admire the view your father was so thoughtful to take us to."

Because cars didn't walk but rolled is why they needed roads to get anywhere. The whole world rolled from one place to another on endless wheels. The oldest picture of a wheel was found near the Elbe River in Germany. Today there are two million miles of roads in America for rolling on. Most of them are covered with asphalt. Asphalt is everywhere. It's *a semi-solid petroleum product* that lives in the earth and was originally used as glue by Native Americans.

But the really interesting thing about roads is this: They are all connected. Every single one.

After I read Mike's note I waited until it was late that same evening and I set out walking on the roads that would carry me all the way home along a single path. I had been planning to leave sometime soon but now everything was sped up and it was time to go. The campus was already asleep for the night with everyone in their beds weighed down by meds. I knew where I was heading or at least the general direction and I'd packed a plastic bag with a can of tuna fish and one of "chunked chicken." Each of these had metal tabs on them you pulled to open with a hiss. Also I packed some water, a sheet and a protein bar. I wasn't going to walk all the way home. Roads were for rolling so maybe I'd catch a ride in a car by hitchhiking or I'd get as close as I could and then call my brother to come get me in his car. Everyone had cars. The important thing was to be going away from Payton and getting nearer to where I was born. I wanted to smell the green air that used to rise from the lawn behind our house in the evening, and run thumping up the staircase that forever had the plaster archer shooting at it from the living room. I wanted to hear the piano make the music again that was a little bit like a car because you sat in it while it took you away somewhere.

I needed to tell my parents that maybe I forgave them for pushing me out of the house like I was something that smelled bad and had begun to rot.

Or maybe not.

I slipped out the back door of the cottage. The woods began after a stretch of lawn. The stars were out although not really. The stars are always "out" but water in the air overhead sometimes thickens into clouds and blocks the view. The moon shone, though that's not really true either. The moon simply reflects light from the sun towards the earth.

I began crying as I crossed the lawn. I began crying because nothing is what it seems in life including the sky overhead and I was leaving the only place that called itself home, even though it wasn't. Soon I was on a path in the woods. There were many paths winding through the woods around Payton and I'd walked on lots of them. On a few of them I'd also screamed. But the one I was on now led directly to one of the roads. I continued walking and after the tears stopped it was just me doing something I'd never done before on my own two feet, and only a few times in a car or a school bus or an airplane which was this: going home.

The night was very quiet as I moved forward in the dark. I knew that things were sitting on branches around me and watching me as they breathed. I knew that they were burrowing beneath me and feeling my footsteps through the vibrations in the dirt. This was the woods, what it did. I kept walking until I came out of the woods and into a neighborhood which was just houses coming down a small mountain to the road like they'd ridden a landslide. I continued past them and fields opened up again. I wanted to get far enough away so that no one could ever find me and I kept going past more houses with lights going off inside them and more fields until my body remembered that it needed sleep and became very heavy. Finally I stopped at another field that had trees on it and was very quiet.

Above me the sky was almost perfectly clear. The moon was out. A single eyebrow of cloud drifted across its face. I pushed down the grass with my shoes and put the sheet down and lay on it. One of the few times Daddy seemed calm and happy was when he was looking through a telescope at the night sky. Then the cheerful sound came into his voice as he talked about how the night above us that sometimes seemed empty was actually filled with busy intersections of flaming stars and planets. They breathed in space to make light. They crossed vast distances and never crashed. I continued staring at the sky while remembering him saying these things in a slow, calm voice until the earth pushed up into me from below in a way that made me feel I could shut my eyes, and did.

I slept badly but didn't have nightmares for the first time since I'd stopped taking the Risperdal. When I opened my eyes the next morning the little light in the sky made me feel like I was lying on the floor of a big room. A car coughed in the distance. Smoke pushed up out the chimney of a house. I sat up and ate something and looked at my map. Anxiety came back into my head like a swarm of bees but I tried to ignore it and continued staring at the map instead. The road I was on crossed the map as a heavy black stripe but a country road ran alongside it that looked thin enough to sew with. It was about a mile away and would have very few people on it, which was good. I got up and started in that direction.

"These Boots are Made for Walkin'," Nancy Sinatra sang on October 8, 1977, in the Willaway Mall in Darby, New York. Dad and I were in a store called Spencer's Gifts. The salesgirl was looking at me like she was afraid of me. I'd been eating lipstick again. Lipstick smelled like an ice-cream sundae and I always forgot it wasn't and tried eating it again when I saw it.

But that was a long time ago, and even though Nancy Sinatra was probably still singing her song about boots somewhere, now I was a Best Boy on a mission heading home and instead of boots I was wearing sneakers called Converse on my feet. I continued walking as the song faded from my mind and the day began warming which calmed the anxiety-bees a little. Eventually I came to a town called Easter.

You could tell Easter was a town because the houses were closer together. These houses were mostly small and gray. Rusted pickup trucks were parked in their driveways and there was a washing machine on the front lawn of one house. Another had the motor of a car sitting in the middle of the driveway like it had fallen out of the sky and no one had the strength to put it back where it belonged.

Soon I passed a small gas station. The owner was opening the front door of the little building with a key. On his truck was a bumper sticker that said "Gun Control Means Good Aim." He had a beard and was wearing overalls. He stopped what he was doing and gave me a look. I raised my right hand as in a greeting or hello.

But the man only kept giving me the look and frowned.

The whole town only took a minute to walk through. It had a sign saying "Video Vault." It had a sign saying "Mike's Bar." It had a post office sign but the post office was closed. I wasn't rolling but walking but the roads poured me smoothly along anyway.

The next house I passed had the same look as all the other houses but in this house there were children sitting quietly on the front stoop. I was thinking maybe to offer them a piece of food from my pack when their mother opened the front door with a bang and looked at me with an angry look before she swept the children inside and then slammed the door. A moment later I heard the rattle of the lock. Not long after she looked at me from a window with a phone in her hand.

I began to sweat. It trickled a little down my neck and then along my ribs. It was only partly the rising sun. The woman made me nervous. It also made me nervous that a dog had walked up behind me and was now walking alongside me while it turned its head again and again to keep looking at me. To try to feel better I remembered the people who loved me. In order of feeling there was my Momma first who was like the sun I turned towards and then Raykene who touched me with her hands while she put a room around me with her voice along with Dave who was a nice man even if he was always asking me to do things with a cold feeling of instruction in his words. Then there was my brother.

Aside from them, who else?

I was out of the town by now and looked up from the question and saw the telephone wires running alongside the road. Telephone wires ran alongside most roads. They were a highway for voices. If you got close enough you could hear the humming of the voices as they rushed along with important messages such as, *I need, I want, I'm afraid,* and *Please give me that root beer as soon as possible.*

On the wires near me were birds sitting in little groups. I was continuing to walk while staring into the distance when I heard a voice.

"Todd," it said.

"Yes," said my own mouth, before I could think of what or how to respond.

"It's a long way to where you're going."

I looked around but there was no one anywhere.

"It's me," said the voice.

Again I looked hard for it.

"Up here," it said.

I held my hand over my eyes to look upwards. Then I saw the bird. It was tucking its tail into the wind a little bit and was black-colored. On the curving wire it swung to and fro in the breeze.

"Flying is like thinking," it said.

I dropped my bag on the ground which made my spine feel long and I straightened up. I pulled my fingers through my hair to straighten it and my thoughts at the same time.

I looked up again.

"What you got in the bag?" asked the bird in my head.

"I have . . . food," I said.

"Great!" said the bird.

Slowly I looked around me to make sure that there was no one behind a rock who was "funning" me and making the sounds of animals with their throats.

"No," said the bird, "it's me, all right."

"What?" I asked, because I didn't know what else to say.

"I'm starving," said the bird.

When I looked at the bird it had a ring of bright, busy air around it. The bird said, "Seeds and nuts, buddy."

I dug in the bag with my hand and then found what was left of the protein bar in it and peeled back its wrapper before setting it carefully on the road in front of me.

"Bingo," said the bird and swooped down from the wire and walked around the bar a moment like it was studying it. "Things are looking up," it said, and then with its beak it began tapping holes in the bar and lifting its head to swallow the pecked pieces.

After a few seconds, the bird turned its head sideways.

"Grable, New York?" it asked.

"Yes," I said out loud. "But how did you know where I was going?"

"Because animals know everything. That's the big difference."

"The big difference?" I asked.

"Between us and you."

"What?" I said again.

"It'll come to you," said the bird as it continued pecking busily while the colors flexed on its neck. "In the meantime, remember this." It stopped pecking for a second. Its body was live with energy. Its tiny ribs were contracting and expanding and its head was swiveling. Birds were never still.

"Home is in your head," it said.

I was still standing there thinking about what the bird had said when the large whopping sounds of a helicopter came directly up out of the valley and I had just enough time to run under a thick tree and crouch there while it passed nearly overhead. On the bottom of it was written the word "Sheriff." When the sound died away I stayed crouched where I was. I was frightened and didn't move for a long time. Eventually I got back on the road. The bird and the helicopter were gone but now everything was frightening me a lot and the anxiety was making a roaring sound in my head.

"I'm not scared," I said out loud to the bird, but I was.

TWENTY-THREE

THE MISTAKE HAPPENED LATER THAT DAY AFTER I'd finished my food and water. The mistake was to enter a "convenience" store to buy something to eat with the five-dollar bill my father had given me many years ago that I'd always kept as a souvenir even though I never liked thinking about him if I didn't have to. The convenience store was a small building of whitish brick. When I opened the front door, almost immediately it was too bright to see inside. Then the brightness passed away into the distance and I could see aisles and a cashier behind a glass partition with two ceiling fans that were turning slowly.

I'd never been in a store by myself before. But now I was in a store and I was suddenly feeling too tall again and the sickness in my stomach was beginning. At Payton staff always told me to "fight anxiety" by imagining I was breathing a long breath through a tube that began at my heels and popped out the top of my head. "Pop the cork," they always used to say.

But even though I breathed and popped the cork the store

attacked me with fluorescent lights buzzing down from the ceiling along with people's shoes that scuffed on the floor and there
was also the squeak of hinges and the sizzle of frankfurters and
the cracking splat of mustard from the dispenser as a boy in a
denim jacket said, "You shitting me?" which is disgusting, to a
girl who was biting her nails.

I froze. One of the people in the store was filling a coffee
cup with a loud hollow trickling sound. Another was sighing
as he picked up a newspaper with a photo of a plane on the
front page. I took a step forward just as a terrible smashing noise
came through the air and I thought the plane on the front of
the paper had slid from the page and crashed onto the floor but
it was only bells from the front door. I stood whimpering for a
second before I remembered I could leave and I turned around
and walked quickly out the door.

After this the bad phase began. It was a phase of wanting
very much to eat and drink and also suffering from the mistake
of having gone into the store and going out again which made
me unhappy. I was hungry and nervous and I just kept moving
my legs on the road. As I did I sometimes saw a mile marker or
a cross street. Each time I felt a tiny bit better because at least I
was making progress. This progress wasn't on the road, which
looked mostly the same as it had before but on the map, where I
could make a small mark to show my movement. I took the map
out often. I was again walking in an area of fields and few houses.
The wires were there, carrying the voices. Planes went by in the
sky in lines as straight as wires. Occasionally cars passed.

I kept walking on the road that ran ahead of me towards all
the roads of the world. As I walked the air got warmer and I
took my jacket off and left my shirt on. After some time I saw a
van coming. I saw it from far off. The thought that it was maybe

the van from Payton made the anxiety get much worse again and suddenly through the shirt I could smell the special smell coming from my armpits that my brother Nate always talked about when we were kids.

"You're a chemical weirdo," he used to say. Then he'd point to his friends and say, "Derwent and John, get a load of Todd. He doesn't smell like you and I do. He smells like a *laboratory*."

The van came up and went by me without stopping and I now began to walk even quicker because I wanted to get to a place where there weren't dark cars and possible Payton vans and where I could drop food and water onto the beating feeling in my stomach. I was frightened and I thought of Nancy Sinatra and her boots again but this time the song was speeded up in my head because I remembered what happened at the end of the song which was that my father hit me, hard. We were in Spencer's Gifts together and he was buying something for my mother and the salesgirl said something and he slapped me on the side of the head in a way that made me only see white and sent the lipstick flying out of my hand.

"I'm sorry," he said, "but this one would put the floor in his mouth if he could."

I kept walking and was happy that no cars passed for a long time. But then at a certain point I noticed a car coming towards me again. At first it was the size of a pill on the road. Then as I watched it grew steadily from a pill to a baseball to a suitcase to a blackboard. By the time it came up to me I could see it was a dark pickup truck, that stopped with a screech of brakes. I stopped too. The driver's door swung open hard with a very loud sound that scared me. Sometimes when I'm scared I stare at just one point as hard as I can. I stared at the point. The point was a piece of red metal on the side of the truck. The red metal had little freckles of rust on it. I was staring at the freckles when a boot appeared on the stair of the truck. The boot was followed by a torn pair of jeans that carried a body wearing a white T-shirt. Above the T-shirt was a necklace of pieces of metal and bone.

"Well, lookie here," said the voice of Mike the Apron, "what the cat dragged in."

"Unh," I said and raised my eyes while breath poured out of my mouth.

He was shaking his head back and forth and grinning. "I mean, how about that, eh? Half the local cops are out doing the chicken dance looking for you, but this old dog"—he tapped the side of his head—"knew just where to hunt! I figgered my man ain't set up for the main roads. Then I shut my eyes and I saw that line you drew on that damn map." He slapped his hands together with a crack and gave the laugh. "Am I good or what?" Then he stopped laughing. He studied me with his eyes. "And by the way, you look plumb worn out, boy."

"I'm okay."

"I got my doubts about that."

"You broke my stick!" I said.

"Damn straight I did, just like you broke your promise."

He lit a cigarette and held it pinched in his front teeth and blew the smoke out around it.

"What?" I said. I didn't know what he was talking about.

"One hand washes the other, my man. I'm here 'cause I got your back in life, but I need the same from you, straight up. We've been through a shitload of stuff recently, haven't we?"

"I guess."

"Well, that's a bond forever."

"It is?"

"And it's what keeps people looking out for each other."

"You broke my stick!" I repeated.

"Stop beating a dead horse, will ya? Ain't nothing that a broomstick and a penny nail won't fix. I'll make you another goddamned stick. In the meantime, listen up." Mike took another inhale from his cigarette. "Folks may be coming to you soon wanting to talk more about me and Greta Deane. They might be from Payton, they might be from the state, they might be the cops, for all I know. But whoever they are, you gotta zip your lip because *friends don't rat on friends.* That's a rule of life. It's also treason. And you know about treason, right?"

"No."

"People who commit it get shot."

"What?"

I remembered that Mr. Rawson had said I should "immediately" tell him if Mike tried to contact me. But I was on the road in the middle of fields and I was also dizzy and hungry. I looked down at my sneakers. Mike was saying:

"I have a feeling it's all gonna head south because Greta prolly ain't gonna make it."

"Make what?" I asked.

"Die, bro. Poor girl ate her whole chemistry set. A hundred pills, they told me. She'd been storing them up."

"Oooh," I said.

"Sad, yah, but should I lose everything in life just 'cause some head case decided it was lights-out? That's where you come in. I'm counting on you to be a friendly here and lay down some covering fire. If they come to you, say nothing about you and me and Peace, got it?"

I looked around again but just as before there was nothing on the horizon at all. Not a house, not a sign. Not even a bird.

"Right," I said.

"Okay." Mike the Apron smiled. "Now let's talk about you. What you got for rations?"

"What?"

"Food."

"I had a can of chicken and one of tuna but I ate them."

"What else?"

"A protein bar but I ate that too."

He laughed into a hand and then tried to make his face serious. "I can see you *really* thought this trip through, big guy. What was your plan, exactly?"

"To walk for a while and then maybe call my brother."

He made the laugh face again and covered it up. "A helluva plan, yes sir. All I can say is, you're lucky I found you."

He dug in a pocket and took out his car keys and shook them.

"That," he said, "is the sound of a sandwich and a root beer. I'll evac you to the nearest town in the direction you're going and you can grab something to eat and be on your way with a full stomach. Friends, see?"

I said nothing. Mike the Apron pulled down his mirrored glasses and showed me his dirty eyes and then he pushed them back up again.

"Ite?" he said.

I didn't want to go but I was getting hungrier and hungrier and my stomach decided to speak for me.

"All right," I said.

I got into his truck that smelled like him. We were very high up and soon we were going along the road fast. I looked through windshield for a while but when I lowered my eyes I noticed that there was a hammer on the floor of the truck. A hammer wasn't a lance but it was still a weapon. It was even silver like a weapon.

Mike was saying, "Fucked-up part is that she was actually a sweetheart."

"I know," I said. The hammer had the words "True Value" written on the side of it.

"Especially compared to yours."

"Mine?"

"I wouldn't trust Martine Calhoun any more I would the president of these United States."

I'd never hit anyone in my life but I liked throwing the lance into trees. And the hammer was like a lance.

"The president," I said.

Mike the Apron kept talking but I'd stopped listening. The buzzing, hissing sound of anxiety filled my head as I watched myself reaching over and taking the hammer in my hands and then smashing it into Mike's face with the same thunking noise my lance made when I threw it into a tree.

"I seen you looking," he said, and I thought he meant the hammer and that everything was now going to turn very bad and maybe horrible but he only pointed quietly out to a sign ahead of us on high stilts that read "Speed Burger Fast Food," and said, "There you are. That all right?"

Relaxation made my shoulders wide.

"Yes, please."

We found the Speed Burger restaurant which was on the outskirts of a town. He parked there and he said:

"Now, listen, you're having yourself a little adventure and busting out of Dodge and who can blame you. I'm with you all the way, Todd. What you wanna do is stay on the little roads and keep walking east. Eventually the trip'll end but you'll have a hell of a time getting there. You got your maps?"

"Yes."

"Lemme see."

I showed him the map.

"You got it inked already, and all the way home. Shame on me for forgetting what a smart fella you are."

I didn't say anything.

"Todd?"

"Yes."

"Here." He held out a ten-dollar bill and winked. "Call this a down payment on our new understanding."

I didn't want to take it but I didn't know how much a hamburger cost. Also, I only had five dollars. I opened my hand and he put the bill in it.

"Thank you," I said.

"For what? Now give me a hug and get out of here. If you don't see me around next little bit don't worry 'cause I'll be in touch down the road and you can count on *that*."

I didn't want to hug Mike. A second went by and I still didn't want to. But he was continuing to sit in the truck with his arms held wide while he made a face.

I leaned forward and let him hug me and I got out of the truck. It was a long step to the ground and I almost fell.

"On your toes!" I heard Mike yell behind me.

Then I was walking across the parking lot while the truck made a roaring noise as it pulled away. An even louder, brighter wave than the convenience store fell on me as I opened the door of the restaurant, but the smell of burgers was a sidewalk I could walk slowly down through the wave towards the counter. I did and leaned my weight on it.

"I'll have one hamburger and one french fries and a root beer," I said to the woman there. Her name tag said "Daisy."

"And Daisy?" I said. And she said, "Yes?" And I said, "Do you use nut oils in your cooking?"

She looked at me a second and her eyes got small. "What?" she asked.

"Nut oils," I said.

"You from around here?"

"I'm a villager from Payton LivingCenter."

"Kath?" said Daisy to another lady in the back.

"Ma'am," I said to her again, while the person named Kath began walking towards her.

"Yes sir," Daisy said.

"Can I go to your bathroom?"

She gave me the key on a big piece of wood. I found the bathroom and entered it. I was shaking from what had almost happened with Mike in the truck but I like to spend as much time as possible in bathrooms anyway because everything in them is clear and always the same wherever you go and this makes me calm. I used the toilet and then I washed my hands very slowly and carefully and then dried them also carefully using the blow dryer. I was still dizzy from the not-Risperdal and shaking a little but I felt better.

When I got back out to the counter of the restaurant my food was waiting in a white paper bag. Daisy and Kath and two other people were all standing there. They looked at me for a second.

"Why don't you eat that here, hon?" one of them said.

"Why?"

"You'll be nice and comfortable. We set up a table for you, with condiments and all."

"Condiments," I said.

"You know, ketchup."

"Okay," I said.

One of them accompanied me to a table and pointed out to me where to sit.

"Thank you," I said.

"You're welcome," they said and left.

The bag was on the table in front of me and the big hamburger was in the bag inside a little cardboard box. But I couldn't open this box. I tugged on its flaps. I squeezed its sides. But it held on to the hamburger and wouldn't let it go. Then while I was still trying to open the box I felt a hand on my shoulder. It wasn't a gentle hand like Raykene or Dave the vocational manager.

"Todd Aaron?" said a voice. I looked up. An upside-down stern face was looking back at me. The face was attached to a blue uniform.

"Yes," I said.

"I'm Trooper Harold Cullen of the State Police. Would you mind coming with me?"

"Can I bring my hamburger with me?" I said and asked him if he could open it for me also.

He frowned but he didn't say no. After we finished walking out of the restaurant with everybody looking at us, we got into his car and he pointed at the white bag in my hand and in his steady low voice he said, "I don't see the harm in that."

Trooper Cullen opened the hamburger and let me eat it in the car. I sat in the back seat while he drove and I didn't say a single word until we got back to Payton.

Finally I spoke.

"Thank you."

TWENTY-FOUR

"**I**'M VERY DISAPPOINTED IN YOU," MR. RAWSON said, making his jaw long to show his feelings. "And I mean deeply, deeply, personally disappointed." We were sitting in his office and had been for a few minutes. He was wearing the blue box of his suit again. He was wearing a tie. His face had unhappy feelings on it. The phone rang and he picked it up and handed it to me.

"If you ran me over and then shot me," my brother said into my ear in a low voice, "I don't think I could have felt worse than you made me feel these last twenty-four hours."

I'd walked away. I'd been brought back by Trooper Cullen who was a nice person and allowed me to eat my hamburger in his car. Somehow during this time I'd also become "selfish, thoughtless and indifferent to other people's feelings," which was another thing my brother said.

A little bit later I was standing on the lawn in front of my cottage with Raykene. Her hands were lying very gently on my shoulders and she was shaking her head slowly back and forth.

"I may know why you did it," she said. "But what I need to know, honey, what I really, really need to know is why didn't you talk with me first?"

I shrugged my shoulders while staring at the ground.

"What happened to being the sharer-in-chief who told me everything? What happened to our quiet time and no secrets between us?"

"I don't know," I said softly while continuing to look at the ground.

I heard her give a long sigh. "Unfortunately," she said, "there's something else, and it's not good."

A silence began going on and in the silence I looked up finally and saw she was making a sad face. "I just got the news ten minutes ago. The news is very sad. Greta Deane died," she said. Water filled her eyes and began spilling down her cheeks.

"Greta Deane?" I said.

"Called back, that poor innocent soul. 'The righteous perish,' as the Good Book says, though that doesn't make it any easier. I just hope she's found peace." She blew her nose.

"I'm sorry," I said.

The tears made her eyes very bright.

"You know, Todd, I was only four when my mother passed. That one memory I have of her face smiling at me? I just keep it inside me, bright like a candle. When you love someone, it's always too soon, but Greta Deane was only twenty-eight years old."

"Ohhhh," I said.

She looked at me while I looked away.

"It just breaks the heart," she said.

I didn't say anything.

"But the living gotta keep doing what they been doing, and that's why you need to know another thing."

"Yes?"

"Mike Hinton is gone for good."

I felt something turn in my stomach behind my belt buckle.

"Mike Hinton?" I said.

"As gone as a cracked egg. He's never coming back. I just got that news as well. You know, we tried to make you two happy together, but after you left we all had a rethink about things and realized maybe we'd gotten it wrong from the start. I'm not supposed to tell you any of this, sugar, but these are special times, and you know what?"

"What?"

"That man was never on my playlist."

"Mike Hinton"—I repeated his name to be sure—"is not coming back here, ever?"

"That's right. I just got word from Administration. And I'll tell you something else. Mr. Rawson checked out his résumé yesterday, and those medals he supposedly got in Iraq? Couldn't find 'em anywhere. You believe the nerve on that man?"

"Goodie!" I shouted suddenly. At that moment it didn't matter that I'd slept in fields and walked in stores that made me feel I couldn't breathe. It didn't matter that the not-taking Risperdal had caused me to vomit and shake or that I'd ridden in a truck with Mike the Apron and wanted to hit him in the head with a hammer. Suddenly I was grabbing my hands and sticking them between my knees and then rocking forward and back happily as hard as I could.

Raykene raised a hand to her face. She wiped her eyes while she tried to hide her smile. She said, "I know, right? But no perseveratin', you."

Then she put her hand on my shoulder where I was still rocking and said, "Seriously, Todd, steady down, now. This is no time for rejoicing and you got a lot of ground to make up besides. First thing to know is if you ever gonna bust out or do something like it in the future, you'll be at the Dewitt Center before sundown that same day. You want that?"

The Dewitt Center was for "troublesome" villagers. It was a big enclosed building where everyone sat mainly in their small rooms with very few activities and no lawns except a concrete border that went around the building where the residents were walked by staff. They never went to the movies. They never went to the mall. They almost never left campus.

"No," I said, "I don't."

"Of course not. So from here on in, you gotta be extra-careful because people will be watching. Run your mouth but not your legs, all right?"

"Yes."

"Okay." She blew her nose again with a tissue and said, "I'm-a swing by later today and check in on you. Meantime you got your appointment with Sherrod Twist in five minutes to, uh, discuss about what happened. Move on that because you don't wanna be late, right?"

"Right," I said.

Raykene stood looking up into the sky for a moment. "What a world," she said softly. "What a world this is we live in."

I watched her walk away and then I slowly turned in the direction of Sherrod Twist's office. Everyone dislikes Sherrod Twist and I do too. She's the psychiatrist who prescribes your meds. Also she's the person you see when you've done something so bad that Annie Applin can't fix it. I began walking across campus to her office but I wasn't thinking about Sherrod

Twist as I went. I wasn't thinking about Martine who I'd forgotten while I was on the road and then started thinking about lots as soon as I returned. I was thinking about Mike the Apron not ever being there again. I was thinking that it was supposed to make me feel good and it did but that the warm burst of the good feeling was already going away. The voice in my head was taking it away. The voice was telling me that he was still nearby. It was telling me he could still drive his truck into Payton late one night through the open gates and no one would stop him. It was telling me he could come into my unlocked cottage and lean close to my face, drawing his lips back over his rusty yellow teeth and hissing like the nightmare people in my head.

It had been ten days since I'd taken Risperdal and suddenly I wanted it again. I wanted the roof it made. I wanted it to muffle the voice in my brain. When I took Risperdal I could hear that voice but like it was coming through a wall. The walking in fields and stores and the policeman talking and the man in the gas station looking and the everything else that had happened in the last day and a half made me fight to stay calm as I crossed the lawn. I did this by remembering to breathe. Soon I was entering the front door of the building and climbing the stairs.

As I walked into her office Sherrod Twist looked up at me from her desk and smiled with the narrow sides of her face. She's a tall low-voiced woman who's always able to see what you're thinking and I got ready to hear her say, "You stopped taking Risperdal and look what happened."

But instead she said, "Todd, sit down."

"Thank you," I said.

She said nothing. She just looked at me.

Then she looked at me some more.

"Well," she said quietly.

I didn't say anything.

"Quite the little adventure," she said.

"Yes."

"A selfish adventure, don't you think?"

"I don't know."

I was looking up at a far corner of the wall. The lines that made up that corner went on to infinity, shooting out past the stars and planets. I heard her click a pen and take out a piece of paper.

"Well how would *you* describe putting the entire Day Program in jeopardy because you felt like taking a walk? Let's talk about your motives, Todd."

"What?"

"Why'd you do it?"

"I wanted to go home."

"So I gather. What were you planning to do there?"

"I wanted to see my home and my parents."

"You wanted to 'see' your parents? See them how?" She looked at me and frowned. "They died several years ago, as I don't need to tell you, Todd."

I shrugged my shoulders, raising my glance over her frowning face and again looking at the far corner of the wall. Corners were comforting, like bathrooms.

"I don't know."

"I advise you to try to enter as fully as possible into the spirit of this conversation."

"Okay."

"Let's be honest with each other. Obviously your relationship with Mike Hinton was putting you under a lot of strain. We understand that now. We know this was a less-than-optimal situation. In weighing how to respond to what you've done we'll certainly be factoring that in. Institutions can self-correct just like people, you know. I want you to understand that. Todd?"

"Yes."

She leaned back in the chair and she watched me with her little green eyes.

"For how long exactly were you planning your . . . excursion?"

"I'm not sure."

"Are you really not sure?"

I looked over her head.

"Yes."

"I ask because in staff reports your roommate Tommy Doon says something about you having maps and plans and so forth a few weeks ago. So I can assume, Todd, you've been thinking of it at least that long?"

"Uh-huh."

"The answer, then, is 'a good long while.'"

"Maybe."

"I'm not sure I see the maybe here, Todd. I'm not sure I see the maybe anywhere in this room."

There was another silence. I kept feeling like I wasn't saying the right thing but I didn't know what the right thing was. For help I looked at the part of my hand that had the big red welt on it from biting. I could feel the hand telling me it should come into my mouth.

"You have been an outstanding member of this community for a very long time," I heard her say. "There's a reason you're known around here as a 'village elder.' You've been an exemplary resident here and in certain ways even a role model. This is why what you did is all the more disappointing."

"Yes," I said. I was waiting to hear what the threat would be. There was always a threat with Sherrod Twist. It always arrived at the end of other things. She was sitting up in her chair and clearing her throat when I saw Martine out the window and suddenly there was an orange mist in my head and I couldn't hear what Sherrod Twist was saying any longer because all of me had just jumped through my eyes out the window. Martine was walking behind a building and laughing with a higher-functioning Developmental named Randy Atkins. I knew Randy. He used to tease me about holding my mouth open. He wore nice clothes that his parents sent him. He spoke a lot and took pictures with a camera and showed them in the Main Hall on campus. The window I was looking through seemed to move backwards and away from me until the light of it was coming towards me down a long corridor. When I heard my name called I turned away from the window but the corridor stayed in front of my eyes. At the end of the corridor I could see Sherrod Twist's mouth opening and shutting slowly.

"We're going to need to do some evaluations and possibly revisit your meds," she was saying. "Also, there'll be a General Meeting the day after tomorrow to talk about Greta Deane where I'll expect to see you."

A General Meeting was held every year or two when something very serious like a death happened. Everybody went, including even cleaning staff.

"Okay," I said slowly.

"Todd, are you all right?"

"Um, can I go to the bathroom?"

All I wanted was the clear, clean ideas of the sink, the toilet, the white tiles, the pink ball that dispensed the soap. I could feel my heart beating hard. Sherrod Twist was frowning.

"You know where it is," she said.

TWENTY-FIVE

AFTER LOOKING AROUND CAMPUS FOR HER, I SAW her later that day. She was bent over slightly and her mouth was open. Her hair looked chopped again. I was walking towards her on the lawn and I thought she didn't see me, but as I got closer Martine suddenly looked up and made a quick movement of her head in the direction of a space between two buildings. I followed her there and when we were out of sight she straightened up and shut her mouth while the eye that had been drooping suddenly opened wide.

"You!" she said and smiled.

"Hi, Martine."

"You're famous!" she said.

"I walked along a road for two days and then the police brought me back."

"Everybody's talking about you and the dead girl and that man you introduced me to who they threw out of here and I mean *everybody*."

"Greta Deane and Mike Hinton."

"I was dead once too."

"Do you like Randy Atkins?"

"It was boring being dead. My heart stopped. Then it started again. Once I walked away from a facility too. It was called Naismith. They came and got me and shaved my head and put me in a locked ward. Randy Atkins is funny."

"No one likes Randy Atkins."

"Afterwards I thought I was going to get the juice." She made a face of open mouth and wide-open eyes. "You know: buzz buzz!"

"Not even staff likes him," I said.

The eye squinted at me. "Why'd you run away?"

I shrugged my shoulders. "I wanted to go home."

"Are you taking the pills?"

"No."

"Me neither but no one knows. So in public I'm all"—she slumped and her mouth hung open and even her eyelid slid partly down over her eye—"like I'm still on meds. But when I'm alone, I'm all"—she stood up straight and shut her mouth and she flashed the bright eye at me and said, "normal, see?"

I was so surprised I couldn't say anything for a second.

"You can do that?" I asked.

She smiled a big smile.

"You know a lot for a mental," she said, "but also you really don't know anything."

"Thank you," I said. "Are you going to the General Meeting the day after tomorrow?"

"Only because we have to. But can you do me a favor, Todd?"

"What?"

"Get a haircut."

I touched my hair. "A haircut?" And then I remembered that she'd asked me that the first time she'd met me.

She leaned close, then closer.

"Because my parents are coming to take me to lunch and I'd like to take you instead of Randy Atkins, but the way you look now," she started to say when her mouth suddenly fell open and her head fell forward, her eye drooped and she made a sound from her throat that wasn't a word. From over my shoulder I heard someone say, "There you are! I've been looking all over for you! We're late for knitting."

From her open mouth Martine made the sound again. The sound was, "Nguh."

"Nguh," she said, and shuffled slowly by me towards a staff named Connie and I watched the two of them walk away, with Connie stopping every few feet to let Martine catch up.

I went back to the cottage. It had always felt like just another place to stay but walking around on roads with cars going by and sleeping at night in a field made it feel that it was *my* cottage, more than ever before. Tommy Doon was away with his parents and I had the rest of the day off. I turned on the oldies station and lay down on my bed. I was flicking the fingers of my right hand while listening to Robert Goulet singing "Once I Had a Heart" when the phone rang on the living room wall. I slowly got up from the bed to pick it up.

"Hi," I said.

There was a long pause. "Where to begin?" my brother said in a low voice.

"Hi," I said again and remembered that my brother had told me he was going to call me back soon for a "real conversation." During the phone call from Mr. Rawson's office he'd started slow but then began talking very quickly. I hadn't understood a lot of what he had to say except that he was angry and also "humiliated" and also "quite frankly, stunned."

"Todd," he said quietly.

"Yes."

"I think I owe you an apology," he said.

"An apology."

"Yeah, for underestimating how upset this guy made you. You told me but I chalked it up to new-shoe squeaks and that was my bad."

"It's okay," I said. I was still flicking the fingers of one hand. They were attached to my body but were part of my body. This thought surprised me suddenly and I slowed the flicking down so that I could watch better.

"You know what, actually? It's not okay. There are things that I can't talk about, but let's just say that I'm under a lot of stress these days. Be happy you don't know a bottom line from a fruit pie, Todd. Be happy you never even heard the word "externalities." What I'm trying to say," my brother sighed, "is that I wanna make it right."

"Okay," I said, "but Nate?"

"The answer to your question is yes, Todd."

My fingers suddenly stopped moving.

"What?"

There was a long pause.

"Earlier this morning I had a long call with your people," he said. "A good call, a real air-clearer. It helped me see your little walkabout as the cry for help it was. Well, I'm bringing it. Right after that call this morning we sat down and had a family meeting, Beth, me and the kids. The boys are a little older, you know, and I think we're all wiser. I really pressed Beth in particular and I guess what I'm saying is this: we'd like to invite you back."

"*Home?*" I said. "*I can come home?*"

"We could have you out and maybe tour some of the places we used to go as kids in the area. You know, Ting-a-ling's Pizza with the giant pepperoni slices or the Leaning Tower of Szechuan—a trip-down-memory-lane kind of thing."

I began feeling the breath going in and out of me quickly. "Really?" I said.

"I'm betting you're old enough to keep your nose clean, and as I say, the kids would really like to get to know their uncle."

My voice was getting higher still. I couldn't control it.

"When?" I said.

"Tubers?"

"Yes."

"Let a little air out of those tires, please."

I started breathing again.

"Okay," I said.

"I'm thinking very soon, like this weekend."

"Yayyyyy!" I yelled.

"I thought you'd be happy."

"I am happy!"

"Well, so are we."

He said something and then so did I and then he said something else and hung up while I was still talking. But I didn't care. I was going home. I would be taking a plane that went along a kind of high, curved road in air and ending up at the door of the place I was born in before walking through the rooms where Momma's mouth once said things like, "You're the most special person in the whole world." And, "Look at how beautiful the sun is on the leaves today!" And, "It stings, manikins, and then the sting goes away." I spent a long time after the phone call with my brother alone in my room, my hand in my mouth, rocking hard and fast to keep up with all the new feelings. The feelings shot away from me in every direction. I flung myself so far forward after them that I almost fell onto my knees and then so far back that I almost tipped over. As I did this I said the word, "Yah!" again and again. "Yah!" I said, trying hard to keep the feelings in view as they went away over the edge of the horizon and I galloped after them as fast as I could.

TWENTY-SIX

THE GENERAL MEETING WAS HELD IN THE MAIN Hall. Everyone was there and someone had filled the stage with pictures of Greta Deane that were projected very large on a screen. So there was Greta Deane with her hair short. And also with her hair long. And smiling. Or looking down in a shy way that showed her eyelashes. Or staring at a parakeet on her finger while laughing. Or shaking that same finger at someone but not like she was really angry.

She was alive in these pictures. But like my parents she'd already returned to that place I didn't know she'd come from till she went back there forever, which was Death. When I was a little boy I thought Death was where bodies were sent to be changed like coats by the smaller, deeper parts of people called their "spirits." Bodies were brought by these spirits and put on and then dropped again when people died and the body was sent back to Death to be recycled like the things in the compost heap my Daddy used to keep inside a ring of stones in the forest behind the swingset. It was filled with hay and coffee grounds and old eggs and paper that rotted with a sweet smell. But it made heat. It made a lot of heat, even in the winter. It sent steam into the cold air. Like a living body.

Also, many of my staff went away forever and that was like a death too except they sometimes sent you postcards. In all the therapeutic communities staff were always leaving. They were leaving to "raise a family" or join the Army or go back to school or get a better job. First they touched you on the shoulder and asked you to step into the living room or a quiet space for a "tough conversation." Then they cried as they said goodbye. They smiled lots. They hugged you very tight. Then you never saw them again. That's what happened with Curtis and Rhonda and Leshawn and Duane, and also with Katie and Bob and Clarence and Latifa who went away forever like a death even though it was only changing states or cities.

Mr. Rawson was in charge of the meeting. He walked onstage wearing his blue suit and looking serious. He took his place and tapped on the microphone while I looked around the room. Two years earlier a maintenance man had a heart attack and drowned in Payton Pond and that was the last time I'd seen the Main Hall so full. All the villagers were there and all the staff too. The men from Physical Plant sat together wearing blue overalls. The daystaff, the secretaries and cleaners, the security guard and administrators sat in different places and the villagers themselves were divided a little bit into the BI's and everyone else. The BI's mostly sat in separate bleachers and had more staff with them than the Developmentals because they have a harder time following orders. Several of them were wearing mouth guards and a few of them also had modified football helmets and one had a padded shirt on that kept his arms pinned. In the bottom row on the ground level were several adults who dressed like they were going out to dinner and sat very carefully with their hands on their laps. These were parents.

I was seated halfway up next to Raykene who must have been nervous because she kept saying, "All right," and "Here we are," and "There you go," as people went by us to take their seats. On the other side of her was Tommy Doon who had returned from his trip with his parents and barely said hello to me. He seemed very angry about something.

"Good afternoon, villagers, staff and friends," Mr. Rawson said into his microphone, "and welcome to this special plenary meeting of the Payton community."

"Good afternoon, Mr. Rawson," we all said together.

"As most of you are aware," he went on, "Greta Deane passed away recently in circumstances that can only be described as tragic. Greta was a daughter, a friend and a vibrant member of our Payton LivingCenter family. It is our purpose today to honor her memory."

There was a silence in which I began thinking about the soda machine. As we'd entered the Main Hall I'd seen a man in a white van loading trays of cans into it. This meant the machine was full and that my favorite drink which is called Rolly-o Root Beer was now available.

"To that end," Mr. Rawson said, "we'll talk a little today, and we'll sing a little and we'll laugh and maybe cry a little as well. Life is not reckoned only in calendar years but in the quality of its time and by that accounting Greta Deane had a very good life, indeed. I still remember the shy, distracted girl who showed up here as a nineteen-year-old and how she blossomed into an assured young woman who would be the pride of any community she lived in, special needs or not."

He continued talking but I was looking across the large audi-torium. I was gazing past the folded basketball backboards and to that place on the other side where there was a row of people that contained a girl in a black eyepatch. She was easy to see in a crowd. Something flew out of me and shot across the room towards her and was almost all the way to her when it realized that Randy Atkins was sitting next to her. The flying something stopped where it was in the air and fell down on the floor.

"Memory is life," Mr. Rawson was saying, "and that's why we'll have a little help in remembering her today. Clyde?"

Suddenly we heard a sound and saw Clyde Marsh who was a vocational supervisor wheeling something in from the side of the room and towards Mr. Rawson. It looked like the metal skeleton of a tree. It was very tall and it clanked a little and seemed to have hooks on its branches.

"Our Remembrance Tree," said Mr. Rawson, "will host the individual memories of staff and villagers. Monitors will now begin passing out leaves. Later in this ceremony we'll take a moment to write a word or two down on one of these leaves about Greta which will then hang on the tree. A phrase or an image or anything that brings her back to life. The tree will stand in the Main Hall and we'll all have a chance to visit it and thereby remember her."

People began talking a little bit to each other as they passed baskets containing paper leaves and pencils down the rows. Mr. Rawson looked out smiling at the crowd and said, "Yes, it *is* a great idea, isn't it? It was suggested by someone in the Develop-ment Office named Nita Oleska. Nita, are you here?"

A woman I'd never seen before stood up.

"Thank you very much, Nita," said Mr. Rawson. He paused to let people continue passing out the leaves. Then he said, "A person's fundamental identity can be seen most clearly in what they like, their taste in things. To that end, we're now going to listen to one of Greta's favorite songs, suggested to us by her Peace cottagemate Cathy Polhemus. During the listening, let us 'visualize' Greta, thinking of pictures of her in our minds. The music is by a singer from . . . Australia, I believe. Her name is Sia, and the song, correct me if I'm wrong, is called 'Lentil.' I don't pretend to understand what the song 'means.' The point here is to try to draw close to our departed villager. Rob, if you'd be so kind?"

He nodded at someone. Instantly from the ceiling came the sound of a piano playing. A voice of a woman sang along with the piano. It was a very clear, strong voice. Mainly what it was, was sad. I didn't know what she was singing about but I could see the sad pictures on the screen in my head when I shut my eyes. Particularly what I saw was each of my parents now lying in coffins while they turned gradually into giant cigars from the process called *decomposition*. I started to cry. Instantly Raykene's hand was pressing into my arm.

"Let it all the way out," I heard her say in my ear. "There's no such thing as too many tears in this life. And Lord knows, we need some relief around here."

I opened my eyes while the music was going on and I saw that not everyone was crying but that everyone was completely still. The staff was still and the Developmentals and even the BI's were sitting without moving as the piano made its singing sound and the voice sang over it. There was no perseverating or biting in the room. There was no head-banging or groaning or shouting or hissing. The Main Hall was perfectly quiet as the music went into the people in it. Then the music stopped and the crowd began again making sounds of individuals moving in their seats and speaking in little bits of conversation. Several people groaned loudly and Mike Thomaselli, who had been at Payton even longer than me, made his usual two-toned snort.

"That was lovely," said Mr. Rawson into his microphone, "and probably brought us closer to Greta than any amount of talking could."

After that, there were several more events. A roommate of Greta's from Peace House named Connie Anis walked to the front of the room and talked into the microphone about how Greta had always wanted sisters and found them in her house-mates. But then she forgot what she was saying and froze with her hands in the air and shut her eyes tight and started yelling and a staff had to walk her off the stage. Another girl from Peace came up and read a poem she'd written about Greta. Also there was a server from the McDonald's where Greta worked who talked about how "Greta Deane was a femomenon of good vibes who did the toughest stuff like cleaning the grease traps with-out complaining. Everybody loved on her." More people came onstage to talk but I stopped following because I was trying to cross the air towards where Martine was sitting with my mind. I was trying to bend space so that I was sitting next to her instead of Randy Atkins and looking out from eyes that saw her out of their sides and were happy about it. I did this by shutting my own eyes and squeezing every muscle in my body in a way that looked like I was in pain but that actually felt comfortable. Raykene called it "crusherating" and she nudged me in the ribs with her elbow and into my ear she said, "You stop crusherating, now. What are you doing?"

I stopped crusherating but it made me sad to just be sitting there while the bad news came continuously of remembering my Momma was dead and that Martine was having fun with Randy

Atkins and was near enough for him to maybe feel the heat of his body through her clothes.

There was a note a staff read that had been written to us by Greta Deane's parents who were too sad to come. That made some people cry. Time got long for a while after that and ran on without me noticing much about it passing. Then it got short again as it became me specifically writing something with my hand on the leaf of paper for the Remembrance Tree. Raykene told me what to say. "She was nice," I printed very slowly. Soon after that it was all over and everyone was applauding at different speeds or making a roaring sound in their throats.

"I'm going," I said into Raykene's ear.

"Where?" she asked, but I was already walking down the risers and onto the floor through the other people that were now standing up and stretching or rocking and biting parts of themselves. I did tunnel eyes and kept moving forward. But by the time I got to where Martine had been sitting she was gone. I knew I was supposed to go out to lunch with her and her parents soon but I could still feel something buzz in my nerves that was like volts from the thought that she was walking somewhere right then with laughing Randy Atkins. I had quarters in my pocket and I went immediately to the soda machine and slid them one after the other into the slot. The machine threw up the cool can of Rolly-o Root Beer into my hand and as usual for as long as I was drinking it everything was fine.

PART
FIVE

TWENTY-SEVEN

A FTER WILD PETER DIED, THE WORLD WAITED two hundred years for autism to be invented. But then it had to wait another fifty years until autism became so successful it got a new name for itself. According to Mr. C, that name was *Autism Spectrum Disorder*. The new spectrum is very wide. Lots of people who have normal lives and families are "on" the spectrum.

What was once thought to be a rare, severe ailment is now recognized to be a common neurobehavioral disorder that occurs along a broad spectrum.

The spectrum is so broad you can't see from one end to the other. Maybe that's why the number of children with autism keeps going up. Autism is now sometimes said to be *the largest childhood epidemic in history*. The spectrum is called a *comprehensive umbrella term*. It covers lots of things like *Rett Syndrome* and *Asperger's Syndrome* and *Childhood Disintegrative Disorder* and *Pervasive Developmental Disorder* that used to have their own special individual place but now all are part of one big autistic family.

Also, moms are having children at a later age than before and these children are more likely to be autistic. And people are sicker than they used to be because of stress and speed and eating more and eating worse. This makes them take more meds and while they're pregnant these meds can make bad things happen they didn't expect. Some people think it's because of the nine hundred different insecticides in America that are sprayed on food and lawns and parks and that are eaten and drunk and absorbed through the skin. Or maybe it's car pollution because when you're a baby growing inside the belly of someone you're born stupider from having breathed the exhaust of motors. Mr. C says this may be partly why *California has one of the highest rates of autism in the country.*

He says that some people think it's because of *elevated levels of testosterone in the amniotic fluid of mothers.* Or *low levels of the hormone oxytocin.* Others believe that the name *autism* should be changed to *Functional Disconnection Syndrome,* which means certain areas of the brain are growing too fast or too slow compared to other areas, causing the two sides to go out of balance like wheels on a car that make the front of it shake. Some say it's *vaccines* while others say *heavy metals.*

It's all confusing. But that's because words are confusing. And autism is a lot about words. Many of the words around autism come from the *DSM.* Mr C says it stands for the *"Diagnostic and Statistical Manual of Mental Disorders."* It was made by the Army after World War Two to put labels on all the different kinds of mental problems soldiers had after being shot at and burned and maimed and gassed. This manual is now *the bible of the psychiatric profession.* Doctors read it to know what's wrong with their patients and what meds to give them. Every few years there's a new *DSM* with new syndromes and new words for them.

Autism showed up in the *DSM* in 1980. Autism Spectrum Disorder showed up in 2008.

Another thing Mr. C says is that you can't take a blood test for autism. The doctor can't rub things on your skin like the allergist does to see what makes you sneeze. You can't X-ray the brain and see the autism spot. You can't listen for it with a stethoscope.

The diagnosis is highly subjective and can only be derived from observing a patient's behavior.

But the spectrum is so wide that actually almost anyone can be on it. If you're a *picky eater* or *like being solitary* you could be on the spectrum. If you have *a natural gift for music* you might be on it. If you have *a good memory for detail* or a *flair for drawing* you could be on it. Isaac Newton was *the greatest logical-scientific mind that ever lived* and he was on it. People on it don't have to take meds or get driven in a van to work in a high school cafeteria. They can have children and suits and wear watches while flying on planes. They can pose for pictures and act in movies. They are Steve Jobs, Albert Einstein, Lewis Carroll, Andy Warhol. They are sharing elevators with you and cooking your food.

Maybe they're even marrying you.

TWENTY-EIGHT

I WOKE UP IN MY BED WITH A SUDDEN HEAVE. IT was dark and the house creaked around me. Strange patterns moved on the wall. Soon I realized these were made by the headlights of a car driving away. Normally there aren't cars on campus in the middle of the night. I don't have a clock in my room but I knew it was very late. I could tell this by the stillness. Why had someone been on campus at this time of night? I looked carefully around my room, feeling my eyes touch the things one by one. Then my eyes shut and I went back to sleep.

Later that morning after I had eaten breakfast and showered I was waiting patiently in front of my bedroom window. I had been told to do so because Martine's parents were coming to get me. Sherrod Twist had said this was a "probationary outing" and that she expected me to "behave impeccably." I continued to wait by the window until noon when a long shiny black car came out of the sunshine and slid by my cottage and then kept going.

A minute later I heard a knock on the front door. I left my room and walked past Tommy Doon who was watching television. When I opened the front door Martine was standing there.

"Well, look at you," she said.

"Okay, look."

She pointed with her finger at where I had recently had all my hair cut with an electric clipper that buzzed loudly in my ear.

"Mr. Clean," she said.

"Yes."

"Finally we get to see your face," she said.

"My face," I said.

"And you think that's a good thing?" she asked and frowned.

"I don't know," I said.

"Ta-da!" she cried. "Mom, Dad, meet Todd."

Martine's father stepped into the living room. He was very tall and had waves of shiny white hair on his head and was wearing a short-sleeved dark shirt and dark pants. He walked towards me with an arm held out straight in front of him like a pole. At the end of the pole was his open hand.

"Corbin Calhoun, pleased to meet you," he said in a low voice.

"He says he's my father," said Martine, "but we're not sure." After a second she laughed.

"Funny," said a small gray-haired woman who came into the cottage behind the father, "is not one of her gifts." The woman stuck out her hand.

"Annalise Calhoun."

"Hello," I said.

The mother shook my hand and looked at me and then around the cottage.

"Martine Calhoun's parents," Tommy Doon said loudly.

"Tommy Doon is my roommate," I said.

"And the village announcer, I see," the father said. "Hello, Tommy."

"Don't try any rough stuff!" Tommy cried, and looked in a frightened way at the father and then got up fast for a very fat person and ran into his room.

"People say my dad looks like a bad guy from TV," said Martine.

"The hair," said the mother and pointed to the father's waves of whitish hair.

"Don't buy the hype," said the father to me and winked. "I'm just a pussycat."

"Wow," said the mother as she looked around, "and you keep this so clean."

Tommy Doon poked his head out.

"Todd Aaron is a slob!" he shouted, and then he saw Mr. Calhoun and stuck his head back in his room and slammed the door.

The mother looked out the window and said pleasantly, "And people look so well put together here, groomed and dressed."

"Mom, you say something nice about every place I go, and then I leave and it's suddenly the worst place on earth," said Martine.

"Hey, kids, how about some lunch?" said the father, and then he smiled. "Or are my needs at the bottom of the list today, as usual?"

"Have you met my husband?" the mother asked me. "The son I never had?"

The father blew her a kiss.

"Mr. Calhoun?" A man in a black suit and a cap stood in the doorway.

"Hi, Bernie," said Martine. The man nodded at her.

"Right," said the father, "let's go."

We walked out the door where the big car was waiting for us with its doors open and its dark red blood-colored insides hanging out. Inside the car were two long couches in this same color that faced each other. Martine and her father got in one and the mother and I got in another. Through the windows I could see villagers not moving on the lawn from their surprise at seeing a car that big at Payton. The doors closed and we began driving off while pieces of gravel shot out from under the tires with gunshot noises. The mother looked out the windows.

"It's all so delightfully . . . rural," she said.

"That's what happens when you get out of the city," said the father, taking a phone out of his pocket.

"I kind of always wished I'd grown up on a real farm," the mother said to me and put her hands together under her chin.

"Oh," I said.

"But Cos Cob was a bit short on that kind of thing," she said. She tilted her head to one side and smiled.

"I'm leaving," said Martine.

"Thanks for telling us," said the father, looking at something on the phone. He leaned forward. "The Orangerie, right?" he said to the driver.

"Yes sir," said the man.

"Did you Yelp it?" the mother asked. "You remember that last place, what was that called?"

"Le Grand Boeuf."

"Just awful."

"True, but just because this one has a pretentious name too doesn't mean it makes bad food."

"I forget how wise you are," said the mother. "Have I ever told you how wise you are?"

"My parents," said Martine with a smile, "pretend it's fun to argue but they really do hate each other."

"This isn't the time, sweetie," said the mother.

"When is it ever?" said the father.

"I'm leaving here," said Martine.

"No, you're not," said the father.

"Yes, I am. People in this place are sick. They sit around staring all day with their mouths open."

"Remember what Dr. Wolfensohn said?" asked the father.

"Wolfenstein," said the mother.

"Whatever. 'At this point in her life,' the doctor said, 'Martine needs her feet held to the fire until she feels the burn.'"

"He was a repulsive little man," said the mother.

"So what?" said the father. "He told the truth."

"Repulsive," the mother repeated, "like the rest of them."

"Rest of who?" said the father.

"Did you know that Todd's parents never held his head underwater when he was a boy, not even once?" said Martine.

"Now?" said the mother. "Again?"

"Apparently," said the father to his phone.

"Or pushed him out of a moving car either?"

The father continued to look at his phone and then squinted at it. "I do believe I know this song."

"Or gave him brain damage?"

"Yes, that's the one," the father said.

"Please don't wind her up," said the mother.

"Or made him eat his own tampon?"

The father frowned at his phone while he pressed on it with a finger and said, "One bar. O Verizon, how you disappoint!"

"Or forced him to put his eye out with a rock," Martine said.

There was complete silence.

"I think we're about here," the driver said as the car pulled into a parking lot in front of a large white-painted building and stopped. He went around and opened our doors. No one said anything as we got out of the car except that Martine put her face really close to mine and whispered, "I won!"

The restaurant seemed like a very fancy house that people had wandered into by mistake and decided to have a meal there. It had glass chandeliers and mirrors on the wall. It had music playing softly and cold air filled with an orange spice. A woman brought us into a room in the back where there wasn't anybody else. Small metal dishes of oil and olives and bread sat on the table. Martine was smiling at me like I was supposed to understand something as we sat down.

"Todd?" said the mother.

"Yes?"

"I guess my question is, what is it mainly that you do? I mean, what are your main daily activities, you know? I'm interested in the vocational side of things at Payton. I know that Martine spends a lot of her time in the knitting studio, and she's made beautiful scarves for her father and myself, but she's also complained of boredom. Is that a problem for you? And I do appreciate you speaking candidly, Todd."

I tried very hard to think of something to say but I didn't know how to answer what she was asking. I knew what tiredness was. I knew what upsetness or sadness was. I knew about hunger and missing things too but her question confused me.

"I don't know."

"Mom," said Martine. Then she said again, "*Mom?*"

The mother looked at her while I looked down at the table and I heard her whisper something to her mother. When I looked up the mother was looking at me with a smile.

"How are you today, Todd?" she said slowly.

"I'm fine," I said.

"That's so very good. We're very happy that you could join us today."

"Thank you," I said.

"Where are you from?" the father asked, also slowly.

"I am from Grable, New York,"

"Up by Westerville, isn't it?" said the father.

"I don't know."

"And Martine tells us you're one of the, um, longest-serving, or I suppose one would say staying, residents."

"What?" I said.

The waitress came and listed the specials. She said she'd be back to take our order and she winked at me as she left.

"You have impeccable manners," the mother said.

"Thank you."

They were speaking differently. They were talking to me in a different way now that I could feel and that was part of the way everyone had mostly talked to me. The way they'd been before was not.

"Tell us about your background, I mean your family," said the mother in her new voice.

"My brother," I said, "works in an office."

"And what line of work is your brother in?" the father asked.

"He's an accountant."

"An honorable profession," said the father, nodding.

"That's the same thing my dad does," said Martine.

"Not exactly," said the mother, reaching for the bread.

"But didn't you always say you push money around for a living, Dad?" asked Martine.

"Stop it," said the mother.

"Didn't you?" she said. "Like those guys at a casino with a rake who push chips around a table, but you do it with a computer?"

Her father put a piece of bread in his mouth and began chewing with clicking squeaks of the jaw.

"I said enough," said the mother.

"Actually," said the father, "she happens to be right, more or less."

"Anyone can do it," Martine said to me. "That's what he always says. He just happened to inherit a ton of it from his father. We're really rich."

"You already told me that," I said.

Both the parents looked at me.

"I already told him that," Martine said.

The parents stopped looking at me and looked at each other.

"I also showed him how to not take his meds."

"Of course you did," the father said. He was reaching for another piece of bread when his wife's hand on his arm stopped him.

"Cor?" she said.

"Yes."

"Did you hear what she just said?"

"What was that?"

"Your daughter just told you that she's sabotaging everything all over again, and at this point there are essentially no options left."

"I'm aware of that, Annalise."

"Well, is there anything you'd like to say?"

The father touched the arm of a passing waitress. "Miss? A Beefeater's on the rocks with a twist?"

"Yes sir."

The wife folded her arms across her chest. "And now drinking at lunch."

"Evidently."

"Let me say it again. If she flunks out of here, there are no essentially no options left."

"I love this part," said Martine and put her hands between her legs just like I do and began to rock.

Before anyone else could say anything, another waitress returned to take our order. Her name tag read "Bunny." This disturbed me because it made me think of the way animals like dogs and cats and rabbits are actually people crushed into four-legged bodies which is partly why they frighten me so much. I couldn't look in her direction for that reason and to my closed menu I said:

"Hamburger with fries, please."

"We have a ten-ounce filet mignon done with a béarnaise sauce. Would that do?" said the waitress.

"Perfectly," said the father.

After that Martine and her parents ordered. When they were done, the mother made a smiling face that showed us all the cords in her neck. She said, "Well, since everyone is apparently perfectly happy with the way things are and how they're going, I think I'll have a drink to celebrate, myself. Waiter!"

A man approached who had wet hair that gleamed in coils and a white jacket.

"Are you the wine captain or something?"

"I am the sommelier, madame."

"Could you get me a glass of Pinot Grigio, please, very cold?"

"Normally this doesn't happen," Martine whispered to me excitedly.

The sommelier was bowing in a way that showed us the curving part in his hair. "But of course," he said.

The father's phone whistled at him like a person. He took it out and looked at it just as the waitress came back with his drink.

"Don't you love it," he said, standing up and taking the drink from the waitress, "when things work out just like they're supposed to?" He winked at me and then walked quickly away from the table talking on the phone.

The mother's very cold Pinot Grigio arrived.

"Todd ran away from Payton," Martine said.

"Really? How interesting," she said, but she seemed sad as she said it.

"And soon I'm going home to visit my brother!" I said.

"Very nice," she said, but she seemed like she wasn't even listening anymore.

The father came back and the meal went on for a while after that but I stopped paying much attention. That's because when the food came I began eating it and it was very good and could be almost all that was happening to me, as usual. The father's phone whistled several more times and he left the table each time to take the call. The mother kept getting sadder and sadder as the meal went on and she ordered several more glasses of very cold Pinot Grigio. Finally she stopped trying to talk to me and talked mainly to Martine and then she stopped talking to her too. I think she started crying at one point.

The long car brought us back home while no one said a word. The father looked at his phone the whole way. The mother looked at her lap. Martine was very happy and she smiled a lot and winked more than once during the drive. But I'm not sure the parents even said goodbye to me as I stepped out and went back into the cottage and lay down on my bed.

TWENTY-NINE

O N T H E D A Y B E F O R E I W E N T H O M E T O S E E M Y
brother I decided to visit the spot where I'd hidden the
stick. It had been many days since I'd seen the stick. I thought
about the stick sometimes when I walked in the woods but no
matter what I thought I was afraid to actually go see it again
because ever since it had been broken it reminded me too much
of Mike the Apron. But on the day before I left for my brother's
I suddenly cared less about all the things that were bothering
me. I decided to go find it and maybe try to fix it.

I left the cottage that morning and took the path into the
woods. It was summer and there was more light everywhere
than at any other time of the year. The light seemed to shine
upwards from the ground while also coming down from the sky.
After walking for a while I got to the right place in the woods
and bent over and parted the grass. But then I stopped moving.
I stopped because where the old stick had been was a brand-
new stick that was shiny and had a point on it that was not a

nail but something solid and silver and tapered like a real spear. Very gently I lifted this stick off the flat rock it had been resting on. The stick felt smooth and powerful in my hand. But then I noticed that there were words on the rock, written in magic marker, and I bent over to look.

"I keep my promises, friend," the words said. "Now you keep yours."

The stick turned burning hot in my hand and I dropped it with a clatter on the rock. Then I turned and began running back along the path. I don't run easily because I'm heavy and "posturally challenged," says Ferdy Dawkins, our physical therapist. But I ran now. My feet beat on the path and my arms swung and I sucked air into my lungs and I said, "Guh! Guh! guh!" as I went. I felt like Mike the Apron had reached all the way out from wherever he was and slapped my face hard with his hand.

The day was long and after what happened I became very anxious. Sherrod Twist still didn't know I was off my Risperdal and had scheduled a blood draw but it hadn't happened yet. I was anxious as I microwaved my lunch and anxious as I worked in the woodshop. I was anxious walking everywhere around campus and even more anxious as I lay in my bed at night. But I talked as little as possible that day and to feel better I pushed my thoughts at the future whenever I could. I did this by spending a long time studying the numbers and the writing on my plane ticket. Also I looked at a wall calendar and measured the time I'd be away with my hands and then held the hands in the air in the same position and looked at things through the gap. I'd be away at my brother's from the teapot to the stove. Or from the edge of the door to the part where there was a long crack in the plaster wall. In this way I forgot about my anxiety a little bit while the future continued steadily coming towards me. Then it was finally the next morning and I was showered and the future was here and Raykene was knocking at my cottage door. She had come to take me to the airport in the van.

"Glory be but the day has arrived!" she said with a big smile.

Raykene was wearing something that had a lot of colors in it and sent the colors into the air. When we got into the van she put both her hands on the steering wheel and stared straight ahead as she drove. "Life is just a bunch of curveballs thrown by God, my friend," she said to the windshield. "Sometimes you hit a home run, and sometimes the ball hits you." She turned and looked at me. I looked away. "You're lucky to have a family like this to go back to, Todd, because not everyone here does. You know that, right?"

"Yes," I said, but mainly what I was doing was staring out the window as a way of sending myself already home.

Then we got to the airport where planes strained into the air over our heads and I was about to get anxious again from the sound and light but we got out and Raykene held her arm tight around my shoulder as we walked through the giant echoing room called "concourse" and she said, "There's been some bumps in the road recently but everything's good and it's gonna get better. I love you. You know that, right?"

She went to the counter and got a special gate pass to accompany me through security and to the gate where she held my hand and gave me a strong hug goodbye. Then I walked on the line into the plane and buckled myself into my seat which felt very nice.

The very first time I'd ever flown on a plane had been when I was a little boy and I took Pan Am all the way to California with Momma to find a place that was just right for me. It was only the

two of us, which I loved. Momma's hair was shaped like a bell
for the trip and she had on an orange dress and loose bracelets
on her wrist. The plane went up while I watched the earth turning below through the little windows. Frost crept over them.
The plane shook and shook. Momma laughed and I laughed too
and the stewardess brought us food and a special ice-cream des-
sert for me. Then the plane landed and not long after we were
standing by the ocean. The sun was very strong that day and the
ocean threw snapping whips of waves at the beach. The name of
the place we were visiting was the Alta Borda Living Center. A
man named Dr. Harris was walking with us. Momma said to
him, "This is one of the most beautiful places I've ever seen. Can
I move here permanently?"

Dr. Harris had wave-shaped hair and very white teeth. He
laughed and said, "We can talk about that. In the meantime, let
me show you the residential facilities, Mrs. Aaron. I think you'll
be impressed."

Momma held my hand as we walked around the green grass
and white buildings that had people living in them in sunny
rooms. I kept wanting to go sit in the side of the ocean and let
the waves fall on me but Momma was tugging on my hand.
"The point of Alta Borda is to provide a safe but stimulating
environment for expanding the horizons of the disabled child,"
Dr. Harris was saying. "I think you'll find we're truly a kids-
first facility, with a teacher-student ratio that's among the best
in the country."

Momma seemed very impressed. She said, "This place is a
breath of fresh air compared to the residential centers I've seen
on the East Coast."

But afterwards back in our hotel room before we went down
to dinner she said, "That man was crazy, honey. I think he was

on something. He never stopped talking and did you notice how he looked at me?" She was adjusting my collar with little touches from up close and I could feel the warmth from the front of her body coming onto my neck and face.

"No," I said happily.

Now it was many years later and I was running down the runway on a plane just like before but I was going back to where Momma had once lived and died instead of away from it. The plane sat at an angle in the sky for a while before it "leveled out" and the seat belt sign rang. I stopped remembering being a boy and took my seat belt off and stood up. My brother had made "special arrangements" with a flight attendant named Johannes who was suddenly right near me asking in a friendly voice, "Everything good?"

"I need to use the bathroom," I said.

"Well, of course you do," he said, and he pointed towards the part of the plane where the bathroom was.

The airplane bathroom was a small version of the same rooms that I like to stand in whenever I see them. Also, I pee a lot which is a side effect of the meds I take. Once a year I see Dr. Fleming the urologist. He always says, "How's the pipes?" and winks. In the little shaking bathroom of the plane I got most of it in the bowl though some might have also hit the floor. Then I made my way back to my seat and as I was sitting down the girl next to me looked up from her magazine. I looked back and said:

"Hello, Ma'am."

The girl said something out of the side of her mouth to the girl next to her and they both laughed.

I shut my eyes and tried to remember the food they'd served me when I flew with my Momma. It was a kind of TV dinner like we used to eat as boys from a foil tray with our family sitting in the light falling from the television. For lunch today Raykene had given me a paper bag that had a turkey sandwich in it along with a dill pickle and barbeque-flavored potato chips. I took my food out just as Johannes came by with a little rolling cart of drinks. He was very calm and friendly as he opened the tray in front of me to put the food on.

"Would you like some soda or tea or juice with that?" he asked.

"A Sprite, please."

"Coming right up!"

I wanted a second extra pack of the peanuts that came with the drink and he gave it to me. I wanted the warm baked cookie they brought around after dinner and he gave me that too. Johannes kept coming by and I kept saying yes and eating and drinking. I ate while I drank a soda and an apple juice and then a cranapple juice and then three waters. I'm not sure how much time went by before the wheels rumbled as the whole plane slowly fell to earth and the tires spanked on the runway and we were somewhere new.

My brother was waiting in the crowd at the gate with his special gate pass in his hand. "Thanks so much, Johannes, I've got him from here," he said past my ear as he hugged me.

Johannes said, "Of course. And he was a real gentleman."

"Of course he was," said my brother and hugged me close while I made my special smile and he kept one arm wrapped around my shoulder as we walked down the giant hall to his car. "Tubesteak in the house!" he yelled over the sound of all the many people moving, and squeezed me to him as we got on the elevator. Soon we were in his car and leaving the airport on a long curved road that made a hand of gravity press into us from the side before we got on the highway. We stayed on that for a few minutes and then took a side road which ran straight past Roma Pizza and the House of Deli and also Rhonda's Hair and the Square Deal Hardware Store and now I knew where I was. I kept turning my head again and again to watch the places as they came out of my memory a second before they became actual buildings, and shot past us.

"You're acting like a guy just out of prison," Nate said and laughed.

We passed the Rudge Road Elementary School. We passed the Squahosset Reservoir and the A&P. I could hear my breath beginning to go in and out like it did when I was excited because we were turning now onto the hill leading to the house where I'd been born and lived. Soon we were climbing and I was remembering the exact feeling of the hill inside my body and because of that a big wave came over me like when you're about to throw up except it wasn't painful but was filled with something else.

"Drumroll, please," said Nate as we began going past the house that was my house and fit exactly into the place in my head where I remembered it. A different car was in the driveway. The color of the house was different. The trees and shrubs were different also. But the doors and windows made the same face at me they always had and I did what I'd always done as a boy: I made my own face back.

"You look like you got gas," said my brother, turning to look at me.

"No," I said.

"Pace yourself," he said, as we went past several more houses on the hill and then we pulled into a driveway, "because it's a long visit."

"Your house," I said.

"My house," Nate said, turning the car off. There was a

moment of silence. The car ticked. Into the silence he said in a softer voice:

"And now it's yours as well."

I wanted to be happy but the lawn of the house was shaped like a green loaf that the face of the house might be eating with indigestion. Our own house down the block always had the face of a happy giant but Nate's house frightened me. I was still looking out the window feeling afraid to move when the front door of the house opened and my brother's wife Beth came falling out of it with the two children behind her.

"Hi!" said Beth.

It was the second time I'd seen her in my life and she was wearing the same dress that hung straight down from her shoulders. Her hair that used to be black was now light-colored and cut in the shape of an upside-down wooden salad bowl like the ones that were made in Payton woodshop on a machine called a *lathe*.

"Welcome!" she shouted.

"Hello," I said, getting out of the car and looking at her instead of the house.

The boys came up behind her. They were now eleven and twelve and wearing shorts. Their legs were thin and they had large heads. They leaned their heads together.

"Hi, Uncle Todd!" they yelled.

"You made it!" said Beth in a surprised voice as she walked forward and puffed air in my ear for a kiss: "Mwah!" She stood in front of me and smiled while the lids of her eyes slowly closed and opened.

"It's been a while since you were here and we're just *so* glad you've come," she said.

"Thank you," I said. But I was finding it hard to have this

conversation because I wanted to drop everything and run away from the scowling face of this house and down the block to the house I'd been born in and somehow push my body into it and be eaten by it.

"You're tall," said one of the boys and the other one elbowed him in the ribs.

Nate leaned forward and kissed his wife. Then he said, "Shall we?" He pulled out my suitcase and all of us walked into his house.

It was very big inside. Maybe I'd forgotten how big houses were that people lived in or I'd never known in the first place. Also, it didn't look like our house at all. I stopped and looked up. Directly over my head were two more floors filled with heavy furniture and hanging curtains and water draining into pipes and all this was falling down as hard as it could while the ceiling pushed back against it. The silent strain inside the house made me anxious suddenly and my stomach began to hurt. I breathed deep and tried to "pop the cork."

My brother was looking at me carefully. "Steady on," he said, "we'll get you set up upstairs in a jiffy." I was going to say something back but at that moment there was a sound. It was a clicking thumping sound. It was the sound of a large dog throwing its weight against the basement door. The dog began to bark.

"The dog!" I said.

"Kirby is a friendly dog," said one of the boys.

The dog made a roaring sound.

"Let me take you to your room now," my brother said quickly and grabbed me by the elbow and began walking me up the stairs which were carpeted and attached to the house in some special way so that when you stepped on them you could feel everything shake a little.

"Flying is hard on the body," he said as we got to the top of the stairs while he held my luggage off the floor with one hand. "Take a load off, why don't ya," he said, "and go wash your face and lie down and listen to some music or something for a while. Did you bring your radio?"

"Yes."

"Of course you did. Just set yourself up and hang out up here for a bit and relax. We can meet downstairs when you're ready and I'll make the official, uh, interspecies introductions."

He was talking fast again. I liked when he talked fast even if it usually meant he was telling me something that would make me unhappy or scared. He hugged me again very hard like I like it and then he left. I couldn't hear the dog anymore. To not hear him even better I took my radio out of my suitcase and set it up by the side of the bed and turned it on.

I wanted this to look like my bedroom from childhood which had a dark wooden floor and was painted dark green. But this room was cloud-colored and white and gray. Also the view out the window wasn't of the tops of trees that brushed the air like from my bedroom but of the brown side of another house. I shut my eyes against that difference in the houses and pressed the button that made the radio move through its channels. Several stations of people talking went by along with a country music station and a classical station and stations in maybe Spanish and other languages. I kept my finger on the button till I found the oldies station finally but they were giving a long weather report so I turned off the radio and lay in bed for a while feeling my body still traveling on the plane and moving forward inside itself. For a few minutes I shut my eyes and felt this flying feeling. A while later I opened my eyes and walked back down the stairs that shook.

The boys were sitting on the couch in the living room trying to balance pencils on their noses and my brother and his wife were somewhere else in the house so I walked quickly across the living room and opened the door and stepped out onto the front lawn. Because we lived near the top of the hill where the wind blew hard I sometimes believed as a boy that all I had to do was move an arm or a hand to be lifted into the air and then carried away like a bird. Even looking down the big hill at things felt like you were flying towards them.

Very faintly now as I continued standing on the front lawn I could hear the high school marching band on the football field below the house. I couldn't see them but I knew they were there. The wind might have changed because the music suddenly got louder. I extended my arms until they were all the way out so that more of me could touch more air. I was closer to the woods and houses and streets of my childhood than I'd been in years. My eyes were open very wide and I stood on the lawn, turning slowly in place with my arms out, waiting for a puff of wind to lift me off the ground so that I could maybe float back over my house, looking down.

"Todd!" my brother was calling me from the front door. I saw him looking around nervously. Then he smiled in a strange way. "Would you mind, uh, coming back in the house now?"

"Okay." I walked back into the house.

"I thought you were upstairs snoozing or something," he said when I got back inside. "I didn't know you were helicoptering on the front lawn."

"Our neighborhood!" I said. Then I didn't know what to say next.

"Yes, it is, but I think the Fensterwalds are the only ones left of the people who were here when we arrived. Everyone else has fluttered off or died. Remember Frankie?"

"Frankie worked on his car a lot," I said.

His wife had come up behind him. "Does he know?" she said quietly.

"Frankie met an unfortunate end," said my brother.

"Ohhhh," I said.

"He was driving his motorcycle fast and rounded a blind curve, and, well, that was kinda all she wrote."

"Dad?" It was Cam, who'd come quietly into the room. He was standing alone against the furniture and I realized he was twice the size of the last time I'd seen him. He had a large watch on one of his wrists. "Can we show him the dog?"

Immediately I felt the tightening in my stomach.

"Sure," said Nate, "we might as well get this over with. Find your brother, will you?"

The boy ran off as my stomach gripped tighter.

"Relax," said my brother. "I wouldn't do this if I thought there was any problem in the least with dear old Kirbs."

But there was a problem. It was the same problem there always was. The problem was that just like cats or bunnies, dogs were also people. They were people with distorted long ears and long noses and pointed big teeth in their mouths who had been crushed into strange bodies and forced to bark horribly instead of talking but they were still people.

"Kirby is a lover," said Beth and smiled at me as Cam led the animal on a leash around a corner and into the living room where I was standing. The dog looked at me and strained against the leash panting while its teeth gleamed and its pink tongue fell out its mouth. The hot, sick fear shot across my belly and I screamed, "No!"

Then I turned and ran back up the stairs and into my room while behind me I heard loud noises including Kirby roaring and people yelling. I lay in bed and made myself as rigid as I could and put the pillow over my head and strained my jaw just as I had after Daddy took my pants down and whipped the burning stripes into me with his belt.

When we were boys together and Nate got tired of torturing me in other ways he used a dog. My parents let him have a dog even though they knew I was afraid of them because Daddy believed it would "toughen you up." But the dog named Peppy frightened me as much when he was a tiny puppy as when he became a large, full-grown animal with a shouting bark and eyes that followed you around a room. Nate knew how scared I was and he waited patiently until one day when my parents were watching TV in the basement and I was standing inside my room looking out the windows.

I often spent time looking out the windows. On this particular afternoon my eyes watched a cord of water shivering in the bottom of ditch alongside the house. At the very same time a corner of sun shrank and shrank on the edge of the driveway as dusk began. A car breathed in the street as it went by below. A bird flew diagonally across the view. My door clicked open and I turned around in time to watch Nate push Peppy into the room while giving the dog a violent hit with a rolled-up newspaper. The dog lunged at me as Nate slammed shut the door and then jammed it shut from the outside with a screwdriver. By the time Daddy broke down the door I had peed and done a number two in my pants. I'd also spilled blood all over the floor from biting my hand almost down to the bone.

Now I felt a hand on my shoulder and heard the deep, grown-up voice of my brother in my ear saying:

"Oh, Tubes. I'm a total idiot. I thought maybe after all this time you'd gotten over it, yes, I did. But why did I think that?"

I didn't say anything and just lay there silent.

"You have no idea," he said, "how sorry I really and truly am. Todd?"

I made myself sit up in bed. He was standing in front of me and slowly shaking his head. "I'm a moron," he said. "We'll keep the dog in the basement, okay?"

"And the cat?" I said.

"She's about twenty years old and ready to croak. But whatever, the cat too."

Slowly I got out of bed and stood back up. He grabbed me by the elbows where he liked to grab me and he brought a fatter, redder version of his childhood face close to mine.

"You're here," he said quietly, "because we love you. Okay?"

I didn't say anything.

"Now let's go downstairs and get some lunch."

I followed him back downstairs. The dog hadn't been put in the basement but in the backyard from where it was looking at me through the windows. It was a large white dog. The boys were sitting at the table quietly staring into their plates. My brother's wife was looking at him.

"Well, hello, genius," she said to my brother.

He cleared his throat. "Beth made a lunch of spaghetti for us with her special Bolognese sauce," he said.

I said in a loud voice, "I *love* spaghetti," and immediately the dog started barking.

"Boys," said Nate quickly, "will one of you go and put Kirby in his house, please?"

"Dogs know when you're scared," Steve said. "Kirby knows you're afraid of him and it makes him want to bark even more."

"Enough with the teaching moment, PBS," said my brother. "Just scoot!"

"My Daddy calls him PBS," said Cam, "because he's boring."

"It's not that," said Beth and laughed. "It's because your brother is serious all the time and likes explaining things."

Cam said nothing as Nate leaned over and took the big tongs and dragged spaghetti out of the wooden bowl in front of us and put it on my plate. Then he poured tomato sauce on it.

"Cheese?" he said.

"Yes, please."

Beth had hair which she often put her index finger in and dialed the way people used to do on telephones when I was a boy. She dialed her hair and said, "So, Todd, it just seems like so much stuff has been happening to you recently that I don't know where to begin."

"Lots of stuff," I said.

"He's in," said Steve, rushing back to the table.

"Thank you," said my brother.

"Dogs actually like being in enclosed spaces," said Steve.

"Like for example that poor girl," Beth said.

"Greta Deane," I said.

"Because it makes them feel calm," said Steve.

"She was only what, twenty-eight?" asked Beth.

"Yes," I said.

"What happened to her?" said Cam.

My brother looked at his wife for a second and made a face.

"Actually," said Beth, "maybe we should talk about this later."

"What happened?" Cam said again, more loudly.

"Well," said his wife, "when some people get very unhappy in life, it can lead to them doing things that they definitely, absolutely wouldn't do if they were feeling better."

"Did she off herself?" said Steve. He was eating his spaghetti very quickly and some of the Bolognese sauce had spilled on his shirt.

"Steve, I told you to wait," Beth said and made a face.

"What does that mean, 'off herself'?" said Cam.

My brother was grating cheese on his wife's spaghetti and he looked at her and said, "Who's the genius now?"

His wife said nothing for a moment. Then suddenly she cried, "Let's say grace!"

"Good idea," said my brother. "Todd, we sometimes hold hands and say grace in our family. I just kind of make something up. I know it's kind of corny, but we like it. Do you mind?"

"No."

"Boys?"

Each of them silently stuck their arms out on either side of them and all of us held hands while the heaps of spaghetti steamed on the table in front of us. Then my brother said, "We are blessed today to eat this food taken from Mother Earth, that endless source of gobs of green goodness."

"'Gobs of green goodness'?" Beth said.

"Whatever. And we are blessed as well to live in a beautiful country filled with good people who are doing their best to pull together. But we are especially and most of all blessed to have among us my brother Todd who hasn't made it out here enough. Amen."

He looked at me. "Not my strong suit, but that was pretty painless, wasn't it, Tubes?"

"Yes," I said. We started eating. The food was very good. I think maybe the children kept talking but I stopped noticing. Then I very clearly heard my brother say, "He was always like that. Our Dad used to say, 'Todd eats like the storm troopers are coming over the wall.' Hey, Todd?"

I stopped moving my fork and looked up.

"Slow down, will ya, bro? You'll live longer."

"Cows," said Steve, "have seven stomachs including a special one called a rumen to digest their food. That's why the family of animals is called ruminants."

"You're boring," said his brother.

"No, I'm not."

"Yes, you are."

"Boys," said my brother, "if you wanna sit at the adult table you're gonna have to behave like adults."

"See?" said Steve.

"He was talking to you too," said Cam.

"No, he wasn't. You don't even know what words mean. You're just a baby."

"Who ever thought," said Beth to me with a smile, "I'd end up nostalgic for the peeing and pooping phase?"

"You're saying bad things about me again," said Cam and suddenly started crying. Over the crying Steve yelled, "You're putting me with him again. Don't put me with him!"

My brother and Beth looked at each other.

"Guys," they said together.

"You *know* I don't like when you do that," said Steve. "I told you I don't like when you do that."

"Enough," said my brother.

"I told you like so many times!"

Steve's voice was going up and up.

"This is simply not cool," my brother said.

"I told you!" Steve shouted.

"Honey?" my brother said to his wife and motioned with his head to one side. Beth nodded and got up and said simply, "Okay, we're not going to do this again today."

She pulled Steve gently to his feet and put a hand in his back and said, "We're going for a walk, you and I, and we're going to talk about manners and the difference between being a child and adult."

"Big difference," said Cam to his brother's back, and then in a loud voice he repeated, "*very* big difference." Steve started to turn back around towards him but Beth pushed him forward and said, "You're older than that." They left the room and a moment later we heard the front door open and shut.

My brother looked at me and blew air through his mouth like he was suddenly tired. "Sometimes I wonder," he said.

"What?" I said.

"Do you know what genes are?" he said.

"Sort of," I said.

"I wonder about our family's genes sometimes, and get nervous. Remember Grandpa Sam?"

Grandpa Sam lived alone a long time ago in a place called Pilgrim State Hospital that I once visited with my Momma when I was a very little boy. It had many tall gray buildings and in one of those buildings was a little room. Grandpa Sam was alone in that room. Drugs made him unable to talk. He sat in a chair and smiled constantly. Momma told me afterwards that he believed there was a mirror world that projected down from our world and that for every step we took there was a person attached downwards to our feet invisibly taking the exact same step.

"Yes," I said, "I remember Grandpa Sam."

My brother looked at me for a while, saying nothing. Then he took a long swallow of his iced tea and said, "Anyway! Just thrilled, Todd. Just thrilled to have you here. And not only me, by the way. Us. *We're* thrilled, all four of us."

"Me too," I said.

We returned to eating our food and then maybe I was tired from the flight or the dog or something else because suddenly I felt that if I didn't take a nap right then that very second I would fall asleep at the table.

"Can I go take a nap?" I asked my brother.

"Hell, yeah, and for as long as you want. Go upstairs and bury yourself, Todd. Sleep for a thousand years. You're home."

THIRTY

T HAT EVENING WE ATE WHAT NATE CALLS "AL
fresco." This means outside on the deck. The deck was on
the second floor and stuck out into air. Because it was the very
end of the day the light made everything look like it was leaning
sideways. Nate and I were alone on the deck for a few minutes
with the air cooling. He had a drink in his hand and I had an
O'Doul's and we were "just being bro's together," he said as he
winked and clinked my bottle with his glass. We heard his sons
yelling at each other downstairs and he smiled and said, "It's
funny how when you have kids of your own, you begin measur-
ing what they have against what you had at their age, and the
thing is that them having more doesn't bother you, it actually
makes you happy, you know what I mean?"

"No," I said.

Beth came out with a tray of things to grill. She was wearing
an apron and had pulled her hair back off her head. On the
tray were shrimp and also hamburgers and there were zucchini

and some potatoes and onions. When she set the tray down she turned to me and put her hands on her hips. The light was now almost gone completely.

"I just want you to know how happy we are to have you here, Todd," she said.

"Thank you."

"For children like ours, who have practically everything in life dumped into their lap, it's just so important that they get to see something else, another experience, a person like you, who happens to be their uncle but who had to deal with some challenges in life other than, you know, where to find his next video game. I want these visits of yours to become a regular thing."

"Honey," said Nate, "do you realize that I lit the grill twenty minutes ago and it's already about six hundred degrees?"

"Well then turn it down." Beth cleared her throat and smiled at me. "I don't wanna sound like a Sunday school teacher here, but before you arrived I had some conversation with the boys on your . . . issues, and I think Cameron wants to do a report on you for school. I guess this is just my long-winded way of saying that I'm glad that we finally got you in our home again. God knows I've been trying."

"Excuse me," said Nate, "but the boys are here and they wanna sing their song."

"What?" said Beth.

"We do?" said the boys, who were now standing in the doorway.

"Yes, you do. Remember? Sing the rap song for your Uncle Todd we rehearsed."

The boys looked at each other and shrugged their shoulders.

"Sing it," Nate said again.

The boys sang their song. They didn't seem to care that much about it and I wasn't really listening either but Beth was very excited afterwards and talked for a long time about their music teacher and how they'd inherited my Momma's "ear." It was nice to listen to her talk about Momma. Then we ate and the rest of night fell finally and Nate lit the lights and the boys did charades which I couldn't really follow but it was also very nice and fun and I slept a lot in bed afterwards and didn't have any nightmares at all.

The next morning when breakfast was over I walked into town with Nate. He had drunk a lot of vodka the night before and ended the evening mostly silent and grumbling to himself but now he was back to being the other nondrinking brother who talked very quickly about a lot of things. We were moving down the little Main Street with its parked cars and the shiny, repeating fronts of shops. Sometimes there was another person walking but mostly we were alone. Nate was interested in pointing out the shops but mainly I wanted to know about the house where I grew up. He told me the house was now owned by people called the Salomons. They were nice people who were a retired couple. They didn't go out much. My brother said:

"They're really old, and they're also kind of clients of mine."

"Clients," I said.

"Well, not exactly, but they've got their retirement savings tied up in the equities department of a firm I steered them to."

"Good," I said.

"For me it is. I brought them in and got a finder's fee. But I like them, actually. They're sturdy old folks with good politics."

When my brother said someone had "good politics" it meant they agreed with him that the world was mostly in trouble.

"It's nice to have someone carrying on the family tradition," he said and laughed.

I knew what he meant. He meant the tradition of Daddy arguing and fighting a lot about "politics" with dinner guests. Daddy read the paper carefully and he liked to talk at the table in a raised voice. Politics was mainly what he talked about. Once my Momma told me that they were both "socialists" and that's why he argued so much. She said I shouldn't tell anyone. I never did.

"Sometimes I think it's a good thing to die with at least a few of your dreams intact. The old man would have been amazed to see how every single one of his hopes for humanity went into the shitter. Workers of the world unite! As if!" Nate laughed and then his face grew serious. "But let's talk about money," he said.

"Okay."

"You probably didn't know this, but SSI only pays the basics. All the gravy, the trips to the arboretum, your excursions, the group overnights—that comes directly out of your little bro's savings."

"Thank you."

"You're welcome."

We continued walking down Main Street while I kept noticing how the buildings had different, newer signs on them but the shapes underneath were the same as when I was a boy.

"Of course I do it gladly. It's what I'm supposed to be doing. I'm happy to be doing it. You're my brother, after all, my one and only."

There was a silence.

"Todd," he said.

"When can I see the house?" I said.

"The what?"

"The house," I said. "When can I—"

"Jesus." He shook his head and gave a small laugh. "And to

think I actually thought I might get a grateful reaction out of you, if even for a split second. You'll see the house, and soon."

We were now entering the "old city" part of Grable. There were fewer houses and they were set farther back from the street. The shops were Tayman's Deli and Rick's Chinese and the One Hour Laundromat. Nate suddenly said:

"By the way, just to set things straight, you know I *did* try to get you out here many times over the last years, and Beth was just a pill about it after the incident. You do know that, right?"

"Yes," I said. "But do you think I can see the house tonight?"

Nate said nothing but shut his eyes and rubbed them hard with his hands for several seconds before he next spoke.

"Would you like to take a train ride?" he asked.

"Yes, I would," I said, "very much."

We were standing near the train station. The town of Grable is a small town that is connected to larger towns by roads but there are also trains. I love trains. Trains are safe because they always know exactly where to go.

"Can we go on the Green Gauge?" I asked.

The Green Gauge railroad wasn't a real train. It was an open car with a big steam locomotive that went back and forth a few miles on a track when we were boys together.

"That one's long gone, I'm afraid," my brother said. "But we can take the commuter train to the next station and then back again. How'd you like that?"

"Great!" I said.

My brother went up to the ticket window and bought tickets. Then we went and stood on the platform.

"Sometimes I forget how you really are," he said. "But seeing you here makes it all come back."

"How do you mean?"

"I have a lot on my plate right now, Todd. Do you know what that means?"

"No."

"It means I'm kinda tapped out, exhausted."

"Sorry."

"I know none of this really matters to you, but when a man is like that the last thing he needs is—"

But I couldn't hear the rest of what he said because a booming wave of sound came suddenly from behind a curve in the tracks and grew quickly into a train that stopped itself with a hiss in front of us and unfolded stairs out its side to the ground. It was only three cars and none of them was a locomotive. This made me sad because I wanted to see the elbowing rods of steel that push the wheels. Also I wanted to see the faces locomotives make of personal effort like whales that shoot steam out a hole on the top of their heads.

"Where's the locomotive?" I asked.

"In a museum," said my brother, "with a lot of other things. Come on."

I followed him up the stairs into the train. It was mostly empty and we got on and took seats for ourselves. The cars started with a screech which frightened me but then they began moving more quietly past the backyards of houses and of people sitting in those yards at small tables. None of these people in their yards looked at us as we went by. Some of them stood in front of grills with long metal forks in their hands. From these grills smoke rose steadily. We went by a house that had a round blue pool in the backyard. We went by a house that had a car parked on the back lawn with four flat tires and another house with a big window that framed a woman holding a spoonful of something towards someone you couldn't see.

Finally the train left the houses behind and entered a long straight section where it began to speed up while making its metal sound of eating the rails. It blew its whistle at intersections. It was going faster and faster. The view out the window was beginning to blur. This was the part I especially liked because each time it happened I thought the train might lift off the rails and maybe, finally, fly into the sky.

I wanted to be on that train. A special smile came onto my face. The train was going even faster. You could feel the future pressing gradually into your body as the train kept accelerating past the way everything stayed the same. I wanted it to leave the rails and head into that future. I wanted it to beat gravity and become gradually weightless as it flew directly towards the sun. The train went faster still. I made fists of my hands and crouched forward. Perhaps this would be the time it happened. Perhaps I could leave and never come back. But then the train began slowing down for the very next station and I was returned to having the same heavy, identical body as before and the disappointment was large. It was very large.

"What's a matter, Todd?" he asked, looking at me and frowning.

"Nothing," I said, which was a lie.

THIRTY-ONE

Ron Salomon swung open the front door of the house and stuck out his old man's face. At the center of that face were lots of very white teeth.

"Welcome!" he said, pushing open the screen door of the house.

"Well, good afternoon!" said my brother.

"Hi, Ron," said Beth, "and thanks for being so flexible on timing."

"The pleasure's all mine," said Ron. "And you're Todd, if I'm not mistaken, right?"

"The man himself," Nate said as Ron showed even more of his teeth and held his hand out to me. I looked over his head and shook.

"Hello!" I said, but maybe my voice was too loud from my excitement because I could feel my brother lean away from me.

"Glad to meet you," said Ron, "and I hear you've come a long way to see this place."

"I used to live here! It was my house!" I said.

"So I understand. Well, it's a very special house and we love it. Whyn't you come right in and I'll give you the tour? Elsie is at a church event but she sends her regards."

"Elsie's so great," said Beth.

My brother made a gesture that meant I was supposed to enter the house. I stepped forward into the front hallway but almost immediately stopped, remembering. Just like in town, everything around me was covered in new things but the older shapes below them made the memories come at me in rushes of feeling.

"Authentic Valencia tiles," Ron Salomon was saying as he pointed with his old, spotted hand at the floor in front of us but suddenly my father was running down the stairs after me out of the past and I could hear the thuds of his feet making sounds inside my head that were louder than the words being said in front of me. He made the low dog growl in his chest as he reached for my collar and yanked me backwards forty years.

"Not this time, damn you!" my father hissed in my ear.

"Elsie's a whiz at finding this kind of stuff," Ron said.

"If you try to run again," said my father as he shook me in long, regular waves that began at my collar and went all the way down to my feet, "I'll cut your legs off at the knees."

"She's really got a fabulous eye," said Beth.

"That's lovely of you to say," said Ron Salomon as my father began dragging me down the hall to the living room, where he often did his hitting.

I knew why my father was so angry. A minute earlier I'd dropped a telephone on his head while he'd been sleeping on the sofa. It was a black, heavy phone and Momma had said, "A big strong boy like you can bring the phone on the extension cord to your father, the call's for him." He'd been lying on the couch with his eyes closed and his mouth open. As I came up to him with the phone in my hands I'd stopped for a moment to look at him while he slept. Things swam back and forth under his eyelids. His lips opened a little more to let breath out. His nostrils went deep into the darkness inside his head in a way that scared me. The heavy phone had two pieces, one with the dial and one that you talked into. From the part you talked into I suddenly heard a tiny voice say, "If he knew what was good for him, he'd drop everything right now." I let the phone go and it fell on his face.

"Over here, you guys," Ron Salomon said, "is a planter filled with stuff we got from San Miguel de Allende. The native artists are called *artesanias*."

"How beautiful!" Beth said. "My girlfriend Mindy collects very similar stuff from the Yucatán."

"Elsie is the decorator," said Ron. "Me"—he shrugged his shoulders—"I'm just the patron."

"Todd?" my brother said to me.

"Yes?" I said.

"Ron asked you a question."

"What?" I said. I was confused. The last thing I'd heard was Ron talking about his wife. Then I'd stopped hearing and started remembering.

"It's okay," said Beth gently. "Ron was just asking if you'd like some lemonade."

"Yes, I would, please. Can I have a straw?"

Ron went and got my lemonade which he gave me in a tall glass that I sipped through a straw as we continued walking through the house. He showed us the kitchen which didn't look at all like what I remembered and then we entered the living room where all the bookshelves and paintings and little plates and tiny statues that had been there when I was a boy were gone. Instead there was a single long couch and a very large black flat television hung on the wall.

"We like the uncluttered look," Ron Salomon was saying, "and that fancy new television is damn sharp in HD mode. On the other hand, I'm at the age where I like a little soft focus."

My brother and Beth laughed while I noticed that the other thing gone from the room was the Knabe concert grand. This was a piano shaped like a giant lying-down harp. Momma pressed the keys of it to magically make clean, perfect rooms of feeling in the air. Mozart was a room. Bach and Beethoven were rooms also. Each of these rooms had different looks to them but all of them were safe like bathrooms because everything in them was exactly where it was supposed to be as far as you could hear in every direction. But if Momma made even a little mistake in her playing I'd yell at her to please, please go back to the very beginning because if not something terrible would happen and the ceiling of the beautiful room would fall on my head.

"Want me to show you the upstairs?" Ron Salomon said.

"No!" I said loudly.

Everybody stopped and turned to look at me.

"Can I see the crawl space?" I said.

Nate made a sound not quite like a laugh. "My brother," he said, "is a little obsessed about this place."

Ron Salomon scratched his head.

"Crawl space?" he said.

"You sure you wanna go there?" Nate asked me.

"Yes."

"The crawl space," Nate said to Ron, "is under the stairs,

where we used to play Army when we were kids and my parents stored clothes and things. I wasn't actually living here when this house was sold so I'm not sure what's there and what's not."

"That space?" Ron Salomon said. "I think I poked my head in once and thought, I gotta call an exterminator and a guy to help clear out all that junk and get it sealed up tight, but I never did. Right this way, everybody."

He turned and walked us down a hall and then he opened a door and we went down the stairs while he flicked a switch.

The basement room was changed like everything else in the house. The concrete floor was covered in a black rubber that quivered under your feet and the fluorescent lights were gone. It didn't look at all like the place where Momma had taught piano to little children seated on the floor who beat on homemade drums with boiled chicken bones in their hands. Her fingers pushed among the keys and the music came out of the upright piano that was called a "spinet," and she said, "Very good, boys and girls, but concentrate on the beats of the song that are like railroad ties holding the tracks."

I crossed the floor towards the place on the wall where I could still see the faint outlines of the crawl space underneath the paint. When I got to it I touched it with my finger.

"Quite some recall you got after forty years," said Ron. "Here, let me help you."

He came over and lifted the painted panel off. Underneath it was an older piece of the darker wood that I remembered. This was the door. It had a tiny hook in it. Ron undid the hook and the door opened. The darkness shined out.

"God, do the memories come back," said my brother. Then he turned and looked at me. "Don't they?"

"Yes."

"I think it's really sweet," said Beth, "him wanting to see his childhood places."

"I wanna go in," I said.

My brother's face fell.

"In?" he said. "Todd, I don't think you can fit anymore."

"Yes, I can."

"He wants to reconnect with something," Beth said, nodding.

"But it's full of creepy-crawlies in there."

"Nate, he'll be fine," Beth said.

Nate looked at Beth and shrugged his shoulders. "Don't let me be the guy who ruins everybody's fun. Sure, whatever—if it's all right with you, Ron."

"No prob by me," said Ron, "as long as your brother doesn't hurt himself."

"You heard it from the man," said Nate. "Go ahead, then. You want me with you?"

"No," I said.

"You sure?"

"Honey," said Beth, "I really think this is a solo mission, if you know what I mean."

"Right," said Nate, and he made a face, looking at me, "but what about his nice new pants?"

"We'll wash his pants," said Beth. "Will you please stop being so difficult? Go right ahead," she said to me and pushed at the crawl space with her chin. "Go."

She continued nodding at me as I got on all fours and crawled slowly into the darkness. The sound of them chatting behind me got quieter as I moved farther inside. For a moment I couldn't really see but instead could smell the damp dark and feel my knees moving over old boards that were maybe broken-down pieces of furniture. I was looking for nails that if they puncture your skin can give you tetanus which causes lockjaw. Then my eyes adjusted and I faintly began seeing piles of old books that had their covers curved from age and a tricycle with tassels on the handlebars. Also there were scattered towels and some baby clothes along with a pair of oars and shoes and piles of old hangers and some skis and boots.

I moved my arm and touched some of the things around me, stirring up clouds of dust. These sparkled in the tiny rods of light that came downwards from holes in the stairway overhead. In the distance as my eyes kept adjusting I could see two clear plastic clothes bags attached to a nail in a far wall. I knew those bags. They were my parents' clothes bags. The plastic on their sides was clouded but if you looked through the clouds you could see the colors of the clothes below like stones in water. I crawled slowly over to them and touched them with my fingers. They had long zippers running down their sides but the zipper was stuck on one when I tried it. I worked it back and forth for a few seconds until it finally came unstuck and gave a buzzing noise as I pulled it all the way down the bag. Inside were several of Daddy's coats that felt soft and new when I touched them. I knew these coats. I'd seen him in these coats and even gone with him to buy them at Gruber's Men's Shop in Little Falls. But my mouth turned down like tasting something bad from remembering and so I stopped touching them and instead poked around in the bag a little bit in the dark. My hand felt something at the very bottom and I pulled out a tiny purse, the size of a girl's slipper.

The purse had a little lock at the top and when I clicked it open it was empty inside. But suddenly I had an idea and stuck my nose quickly into the purse as far as it would go. I took a deep breath while the faint rose powder smell of my Momma came unmistakably into my head and the whole room brightened for a second and then continued to brighten further as it slowly filled with the warm, perfect light of the sun. Then the light went out and I was sitting again in a low-ceilinged dark room hearing the noise of myself swallowing.

My mother had been holding her breath inside that little bag for forty years. She had left it behind hoping I'd find it and now I had it and her inside of me. I held my breath till my head began to pound and then I let it go with a big sigh, feeling it rush out of me and expand back into the world while a lightness and happiness came to me. I shut my eyes to keep feeling these feelings. When I opened them my eyes were even more adjusted to the dark and I saw a wooden box on the ground, not far from my foot. It looked like what my Dad used to store his cigars in that was called a humidor, only bigger. Boxes have a single purpose in life which is to separate what they have from what they don't. I like boxes. I bent over and opened it up. Inside it were two envelopes. But at that moment I heard my brother calling my name in a faint voice that came from outside and so I closed the box, put it under one arm, stuffed the purse into my pants pocket and slowly crawled back towards the door through the little rods of light.

"Here he is," said Ron Salomon as I put my head back out into the basement.

"We were a little worried," Nate said while I crawled out onto the floor and slowly stood up, "And, ah, he comes bearing gifts."

"How was it?" Beth asked, reaching out smiling and rubbing my shoulder, which I don't like.

"Fine," I said.

"You look like you're covered in spiderweb," said Ron Salomon.

"Let's see what you got," Beth said. I handed her the box and put the purse on top of it.

"Whoa," she said, "check out this adorable little clutch, guys.

Paging the 1960s! Was your mom so stylish? I don't remember that."

"Mom," Nate said, "could occasionally cut the rug."

"And then there's this," said Beth, opening the box. She took out the two envelopes. On one of them was written the words, "To my son Todd Aaron." The other said just one word: "pictures."

"The mystery deepens," Nate said in a voice from television.

"It's almost like," Beth said, "she knew that sooner or later you'd come back here and would find this stuff." She put her hand on her heart. "Is it just me, or does anyone else find that kinda unbelievably touching?"

"What else was in there?" said Nate.

"Clothes."

"Of your folks?" Ron Salomon asked.

"Yes."

"If Ron agrees," Nate said, "maybe we could come back sometime in the near future and empty it out."

"Absolutely," said Ron.

"In the meantime," said Nate, "how about we finish the tour and then go home and read the mysterious letter and look at the snaps?"

"Good idea," said Ron, "because I'm itching to show you the master bath. I'm biased, of course, but people say it's Elsie's masterpiece."

We went up the stairs and we saw the bathroom and the other upstairs rooms that had been redone and thickly covered with new paint and carpet and sometimes new walls. When I stood finally in the bedroom where I had been a boy I didn't recognize it. But I didn't care that much because every few minutes I was taking tiny little sips of air through my nose, trying to snuffle the actual remaining atoms of my Momma from my nostrils and into my lungs so they could join the rest and the amount of her inside me could grow.

We said goodbye to Ron and thanked him. Afterwards as we went back up the hill to our house, Nate said, "Damn, I thought the Golden Years were for lying around and watching your annuities, not gut-renovating. I barely recognized the place. Geezers have been busy."

"Must be those ace investments you set him up with," Beth said.

"There you go. And how was that for you, Todd?"

"Good."

"Good?" He looked at me while we continued going up the hill. "That's it? Good? Give us some milk, cow."

Beth stuck her elbow in his ribs and he said, "Ow!"

"Maybe very good," I said, but I was tired and also I didn't want to send my Momma out of my lungs from talking and so I didn't say anything more.

We went back to Nate's house. It was now late afternoon. The boys were at Little League and the dog was in his house in the yard. I sat on a stool near the kitchen while Beth went to get herself a glass of wine and Nate poured himself a drink. As they did these things I closed my eyes and continued to breathe as little as possible while I took all the memories I could find of my mother's rose powder and sent them to the very same place in my head where I mashed them together like potatoes and ketchup. When I tasted what I'd made it was very good. Nate sat on a stool next to me, in front of the kitchen "island," and said, "Honey?"

"Yes," Beth said from the kitchen.

"You ready?"

"Ready Freddy," she said, coming back while holding her glass of wine.

Nate opened the box and took out the two envelopes and

placed them very carefully on the black surface of the island. Then he turned to me.

"You choose," he said.

I looked down and I saw my Momma's handwriting and the words, "To my son Todd Aaron."

"That one," I said.

"Would you do the honors?" Nate asked Beth.

"Yep," she said as she picked up the envelope and tried to open it for a few seconds with a hand and then stopped and reached across the table for a little knife. She slit the envelope up one side, poured the letter out of the side and then smoothed it on the wood of the island.

"Away we go," she said, looking at me and smiling.

"Okay!"

"*Dearest Todd,*" she read:

Here we are and it's my fond hope to spend a few minutes with you. Remember Quiet Time? This is our quiet time. The world is loud with its same old business of living and dying but there will always be a place for a mother to talk to a son who made her life special because of how special he was.

Beth stopped and looked at me and smiled. Nate was looking at his half-emptied glass that he was turning slowly on the table. As soon as I'd heard the words of Momma I'd stood up and begun rocking slowly.

Lately and I'm not sure why, I've just been filled to the brim with memories. Do you remember the book Quick Draw Mcgraw *and how I read it to you, word after word and you shaped your lips around the sounds and it made you happy?*

Do you remember The Cat in the Hat? *Or subway trains and limburger cheese and the sprinkles you always wanted on the Dairy Queen and how much you loved the heels on my black boots? Why did you love those heels so much?*

Momma used to take Nate and me on the subway trains that poked lights in the darkness and rode along a fixed track deep in the belly of the city. I wanted to know where the subway ended. It was important that I know. Finally she took me and I saw the place where the train couldn't go any farther that was simply a wall. I spent a long time looking at that wall.

Darling, we've always told each other everything, and I'm going to tell you something now. Your Daddy is in the hospital because he has something wrong with how he swallows and it's given him one pneumonia after another and this one is the worst of them all and may be the last. I'm just so tired of it all and getting tireder by the day. You know, when you're young everything terrible is far away but the bad thing is looking at you anyway even if you can't see it and it comes towards you slowly and steadily through the years till suddenly it's in front of you and about to take something away for good. Things end, sweet boy. People end and houses end and families end and everything ends but one thing, which is love. The love between people and especially between mothers and their children doesn't end, ever. Do you hear me? Love doesn't end. It flows like a river through the world. Shut your eyes and you can feel it rising.

Momma died in bed. She died in her condo in Florida watching the birds out the window. They hopped on the lawn while she died listening to the piano being played on the hi-fi by a man named Horowitz. Nate made a video of her that he showed me in the chapel at Payton. She died raising a hand in bed and waving goodbye by slowly moving her fingers like she was making one last run of piano notes that is called an *arpeggio*. Then she stared at the camera until the screen went black.

> *Everyone has to leave life, and there are no exceptions. I'll most likely be gone by the time you read this. But I know that you'll be well. I know it because you have your brother and you have your angels. On a more practical level, you'll have a roof over your head from some things like trusts and so forth that I've set up for you, based on the sale of the condo in Florida. Nate will help you in that as he's always helped you. But most of all I know you're well because from the very first day of your life you've had the gift of going goingly and doing doingly. You were a best boy who became a beautiful man and made everybody who knew you very proud.*
>
> *And because no matter what you'll always have your mother.*
>
> *Who is Netta Aaron.*

Then Beth stopped reading and took a tissue from a box of them on the table and pressed it to her eyes. Some time went by, though I don't know how much.

"A very special woman," she said.

"Touching," said Nate, "yes, it is. But then our Mom always knew how to turn a phrase. Even her condolence notes were poems." He smiled a little bit and took a long drink from his glass and then put it down and began turning it around on the table.

Beth looked at me.

"Your mother loved you very much."

"My Momma," I said.

"And she really went out of her way to protect you."

"That she did," said Nate to the table, "in spades."

"Yes," I said.

Everyone was speaking slowly because they were still listening to the sound of Momma's voice in their heads.

"And I guess I forgot about that condo," Beth said.

Nate looked up suddenly over his glass but didn't say anything.

"I mean, I was there once or twice, but I forgot you ever owned it and sold it."

There was a silence.

"You did sell it, didn't you?" she said to Nate.

"Yes."

"How'd you make out?"

"Fine."

There was a silence.

"Am I sensing some reluctance to talk about it?" Beth asked.

"I don't know. Are you?"

"You sold it and you set up a trust of some kind, a special needs trust or something?"

"Something, yes."

Beth stared at him. "Something?"

"I invested the money," he said.

"In . . ."

"How about we postpone the third-degree?"

"So you *don't* want to talk about it."

Nate shut his eyes for a long moment while he frowned. Then he opened them.

"Is anyone hurting in this room?" he asked.

"What?" Beth looked surprised.

"I mean, does anyone in this room not have their monthly expenses met? Or suffer from lack of care?"

"You're being a wee bit defensive here," said Beth. "I simply asked—"

But then she stopped and looked at Nate. "Oh, wait a minute. On no, wait just a minute. This isn't about the new car, is it?"

My brother ignored Beth and turned to me. "Would you like some lunch?" he asked.

"Yes!" I said.

"Please tell me," said Beth, "this is not about the car I couldn't understand how we could afford."

"How about a sandwich?" my brother asked.

"I'd *love* a sandwich," I said.

"Omigod," said Beth, looking steadily at Nate, "it *is* about the car, isn't it?"

"I'll make you one right now," said Nate.

"Wow," Beth said, shaking her head slowly, "I mean, really? To your own brother?"

Nate put his drink down and looked at her.

"What do you think we live on, exactly?" he said quietly.

But Beth was continuing to shake her head like she hadn't heard him.

"The man is helpless," she said.

"You're living in a dream world," said Nate.

"Helpless," she said again, and then more loudly, "utterly defenseless!"

She turned to me. "No," she said, "*I'll* make you a sandwich. And by the way, it will be one of the purest, greatest, most expensive sandwiches ever made."

"Okay!" I said.

"But how about we do something nice first and clear the air on this special day that's about you, not us? How about we take a quick look at those photos?"

"Um," I said. But Beth was already opening the other envelope and tilting it so that a dozen or so photos spilled out in front of us. They were mostly black-and-white squares and some of them had the month and year stamped in gray on the edges. We looked for a few seconds, saying nothing. Gradually I realized that all of them were of Momma and me. I had seen very few photographs of Momma after I left home and almost none of us together. But I always remembered as a boy hearing her say to Daddy, "Okay, here, snap one now!" Usually this happened inside the house. Daddy often took photos of Nate and Momma on trips but mostly swung the face of the camera away from me when it was my turn. But now there was a shot of Momma walking hand in hand with me across the living room when I was a tiny baby. And of her holding me in her lap and kissing me. And of her staring at me across the kitchen table with a huge smile on her face. In another one she was feeding me an ice-cream cone and in another we were eating pizza together with me seated on her lap and a big slice in my mouth.

I was laughing. In every single shot I was laughing or smiling. She had touched these photos with her hands to put them in this envelope and there wasn't one shot in which I wasn't a happy boy.

"It's me and Momma!" I said.

"Yes," said Nate, "it most definitely is. It's you and her and there's no mistake about that."

"No mistake!" I said and began to rock back and forth, swinging my head in the air and feeling the wind moving. Momma was in me now from the crawl space and in my ears from the letter and also now coming into me steadily through my eyes and the rocking was deepening with happiness.

"What a little doll you were," Beth said, smiling.

"With the exception of insects," said Nate, "nearly all infants are cute."

"What is that supposed to mean?" Beth asked. Then she turned to me and said, "I always liked your Mom, but I'm blown away by those photos and letter, whether she put them down there herself for you or someone else did after she passed. It's something maybe only a mother could understand, but I think I'm going to cry again, forgive me, Todd."

"Okay," I said.

She looked at Nate then and said to me, "Too bad not everything she set up for you worked out as planned."

Nate made his eyes small. "Why are you hitting this so hard?" he asked.

"Because it's sickening," Beth said.

"How about you stop biting the hand that feeds you and feed us lunch instead? How about that?"

"You're unbelievable."

Beth went into the kitchen muttering to herself and began making sandwiches.

"I'm really disturbed by this!" she yelled from the kitchen.

"Take it up with Dr. Klosterman!" Nate yelled back.

"Actually"—Beth came back around to the edge of the door, holding a knife in one hand—"I already have."

"Well, that's the problem right there," Nate said. "I went once and never again. Klosterman looks at you like you're something in his nose he wants to blow into a handkerchief and study."

"You're just scared of what he sees. And you should be."

"Oh, please."

In one of the photos, I noticed that Momma was wearing her red hat that was called a tam-o'-shanter. I remembered that hat. I thought maybe that I'd seen that hat in the basement under a blanket of dust and this thought made me excited. I began to rock again.

"Actually, I think I will tell you what he sees because this conversation is seriously pissing me off," Beth said. "He thinks you're locked into an infantile search for the love that was denied you in childhood and that this has filled you with all sorts of nasty aggression that you can't acknowledge. This stunt of yours with the trust money would tend to kind of prove his point, don't you think?"

Nate drained the rest of his drink and put it down on the island with a crack.

"God, but you and Klosterman deserve each other."

"Well, we've got each other," said Beth.

"You sound like you're having an affair," Nate said.

Beth said nothing for a few seconds and then she said slowly, "Are you sure you wanna go there?"

Nate's face became dark as the muscles moved around it. He got to his feet.

"What is that supposed to mean?" he said in a very quiet voice.

Beth said nothing and instead began humming as she turned back to the kitchen. It was a happy little song. It went on for a few seconds coming from the kitchen before it was interrupted by Nate who made a strange groaning sound that was close to crying as he stood up and swept his hand fast across the table.

His glass shattered against the wall and the photos flew up and filled the air over our head for a moment, hanging there and showing all the different versions of Momma and me smiling into the future before they began to fall and kept falling through the quiet air of the room.

PART
SIX

THIRTY-TWO

RAYKENE SAYS I'M THE LUCKIEST PERSON IN THE whole world. She says it's because of how many people there are around me who love me. She says that love and work are the "pillars of life" and that whenever I have doubts about how much I'm loved, all I have to do is open my eyes. She got special permission from Administration to place the happy photos of Momma and me from the crawl space directly on my wall and to put the purse on a little shelf below it. She and a new program associate named Marie did the project, using a special glue that wouldn't hurt the old photographs. So now whenever I want I can lie in bed and turn the lights on and look at the pictures and purse and feel the special feelings. Raykene calls it my Love Wall. She says it's my "very own stairway to Heaven." She thinks it's one of the nicest things she's ever done at Payton and she sometimes asks me if Ambassadors can bring new villagers to see it. I always say yes.

The really good news is that not long after I returned from

visiting my family they moved Tommy Doon out of my cottage and somewhere else on campus where I rarely see him anymore. Raykene said, "Sometimes the chemistry just isn't right, but I think we've got a good match for you this time." My new roommate is named Alex Farmer. He's a Developmental, like me, and quiet and friendly. I'm teaching him to clean the house and also how to use the library, though he really doesn't like to read.

But the very first thing that happened when I returned was that Sherrod Twist finally drew my blood and discovered that I wasn't taking my Risperdal and got "extremely concerned." She asked me what I'd been doing with the pills and I told her I'd been flushing them down the toilet and she called Mr. Rawson and she also said to me, "There will be consequences."

There haven't been so far but she put me back on the dose I was taking before and has started doing weekly blood draws to make sure I'm staying on it. I'm tired again like I used to be but I don't mind.

Also, Martine left. She seemed to think it was very funny that she'd failed at yet another community. She said that "at least my parents are miserable about it, which is something." She said, "You and me, we'll always have Mr. Breeze." On her last day she gave me a long hug, which I liked very much, and then the same shiny black car came to pick her up. This time her parents weren't there but Bernie the driver remembered my name. Martine stuck her head out of the window as the car went away and yelled that she'd be in touch soon but it's now been three months and I haven't heard from her again and am trying to remember as many details as I can about her even though I'm beginning to forget.

I'm beginning to forget lots of things. They seem to be stepping away from me all the time. The oldest memories are still safe in my head. But everything new just keeps falling off. I can't hold it in my brain. I can remember sitting at the beach as a boy while the little waves came up to me and dropped at my feet and I can remember how I was more interested in the moment when the water went away from me with a steady withdrawing sound, heading back to itself. That's the sound I hear all the time now. It's going out faster than it's coming in. Memories are leaving me constantly of trees and words, sounds and feelings, faces and facts and even the tastes of food. Whatever it is, if it happened recently I can't remember it. "I'm not sure," I say when people ask me about something I did the week before. "I can't recall," I say. I just shrug my shoulders.

The good part is that I think my forgetting is helping me feel calmer. I haven't bitten my hand in a long time and have been working hard at the Demont High School cafeteria. Louise found a small newspaper article about me and my "escape" and pinned it to a cabinet near the meat slicer. She teases me and calls me her "ex-con," but I know she's only funning and I make my fake laugh at her and return to chopping onions or dishing out the Sloppy Joes for the students who are always hungry, which makes me happy.

Beth calls every weekend and she always talks about what a great trip it was and how important it was for Cam and Steve to see me and how they ask about me all the time. Also she asked for a photo of my Love Wall which Raykene sent her and she said it's very beautiful and that I made my Momma very happy. Beth said that she and Nate are living apart but that it's just an experiment and they might live together again. She always says that Nate will be calling me soon even though he calls less than ever and also that she's very proud of me and how well I'm doing. I'm an inspiration to her, she says, and next time I come out to visit my family there's lots and lots of people she wants me to meet.

Nobody still really knows what's wrong with me although the words to describe it never stop coming. Mr. B used to have clear, specific ideas about what might be wrong but just type the word "autism" into a computer today and see what happens. But I don't spend as much time on the computer as I used to. More and more it moves too fast for me, like television. Lots of things seem to be moving fast now and the thing moving fastest is time itself. I feel the pillow under my face waking up and then I feel it again when I'm going to sleep and I ask myself: What just happened? Which direction was the day going that just took place?

Every day at least a little bit I continue to wonder where my Momma went because I still can't understand it and it feels like a cheat. But neither Mr. B nor the computer has the answer. I can't figure out where the notes went that she pressed into the air from the piano, or how her voice that is a kind of moving air went through my ears and left forever. Sometimes I think I'm forgetting about other things on purpose so I can concentrate better on the remaining memories I have of her in my head and on the atoms left in my lungs.

One other thing is that I haven't seen or heard from Mike the Apron. I'm trying not to think about him and I'm hoping that eventually I can get good enough at forgetting to forget him completely. Mostly I'm glad about what happened since he came here and I got frightened of him and walked away and tried to go home. "The strong are given more to bear than the weak and learn from the challenge," Raykene says. Raykene says a lot of things like that. She has a round face and very white teeth and breath that smells like cinnamon. She says I've come a long way in life. She says that I was made in God's image and that I "reflect the beauty of his creation." She's trying to get me to go to church again and I like going but maybe because of the Risperdal I more and more just wanna stay home and listen to music when I have Free Time.

I'm listening to music right now. I'm listening to Sérgio Mendes and Brasil '66. He's playing "The Look of Love" and a woman is singing. It's almost night out the windows and the rest of the campus is quiet. You can see the other cottages lighting up with other villagers in them. Alex Farmer is listening to his headphones in his room and I'm listening to headphones in mine. Another day has gone by. Where did it go? I have a feeling it went away to the same place as my parents. Every day the light comes down from the sky and every day it's pulled back again. Daddy always said that space, the stars and planets are a perfect machine. But Mr. B says that the universe is also dying and slowing down. If these are both true then that's another trick. I forgot to look for the compost heap when I went back to my house but I'm sure it's still there somewhere in the backyard. I'm sure it's still turning dead garbage into warmth that's alive. "Your father," Momma said after Daddy died, "vanished into the mystery we live with every day." I hope that Death isn't the end of everything. Or if it is, that it's the kind of end where we can all still be together and look back anyway even if we can't make ourselves heard by the people who are still living. Maybe the dead are all there in one place, crowded in an invisible giant heap stretching all the way up into the sky and leading back to the very first person. Maybe every time we have a memory of someone gone it's because they're yelling something at us that very moment from Death. I hope the train lifts off the track one day and takes me there. I can't stop remembering what happened to me long ago, but that's all right. I don't mind. I was a Best Boy and a good little camper and now I'm a lucky man. Somebody always loved me. That's what Raykene says. She says it all the time. And the thing about Raykene is, she's always right.

ACKNOWLEDGMENTS

To Betsy Lerner, again, for her peerless ear and heart. To Bob Weil, editorial magus, for his acumen and unstinting support. To those in whose homes I wrote: Nevine and Steve Michaan, David Kriegel and Cynthia Flynt, Amy Kaufman and Robert Boyd. To early readers: Susan Bell, Esther Fein and Mark Kamine. Most of all to Lisa Green, for love.

ABOUT THE AUTHOR

Eli Gottlieb is the author of the novels *The Boy Who Went Away*, which received the Rome Prize of the American Academy of Arts and Letters and the McKitterick Prize of the British Society of Authors; *Now You See Him*, which was translated into a dozen languages; and *The Face Thief*. He lives in New York City.